Eve

Jay M. Horne

2018

Bradenton, FL

Jay M. Horne

The Pangea Chronicles

Martha D. Horne, Cover Artist

Janet Vittorio Corica, Pre-production Editor

Cindy L. Martin, Post-production Editor

Martha D. Horne, Illustrator

Cataloguing Publication Data

Horne, Jay M., 1980-

Eve / Jay M. Horne

ISBN: 978 0 9963227-3-7
Library of Congress Control Number: 2018911409

Bookflurry.com

Bradenton, FL

For

Mom,

and those who don't mind getting their sandals a bit dirty.

I

London 1980

It was early October in London. The snow fell from the eaves of the tavern where Jesse had been watching the local news while enjoying his hearty dark lager. The bitterness of the heady brew always seemed to warm him on days such as this. The year was 1980, long before his memory would falter. A time when a black man was not so rare a customer in a place like this, as it once was.

The whites in his eyes and on his palms blended so well with the grays and browns of his skin, one would do well to spare a mention of his ethnic background. All in all, he was a distinguished and obviously wealthy man, with the kind of eyes that didn't linger too long on any one object or person. However, when those dark blue windows to his soul settled on someone, they would feel his gaze powerfully emanate from beneath his thin, well-groomed eyebrows that formed as inverted check marks high on his brow.

It would be in this London tavern, built eloquently out of carved and aged redwood, among the mirage of neon glow along a bar's lacquered surface, that Jesse would have yet another startling revelation. A revelation that would only add to the utter grief and misery that he had so far known as the collection of his memories.

The top hat, which matched so well his suit coat, pants and shoes, now sat in his lap. You normally couldn't catch him in such a get-up, but he was determined to stay in town this time for at least a week. More often than not, he lounged in a sweat suit, but not of the cheap variety by any means! Spending money was one of the only things that brought him true happiness these days, apart from discovering something truly spell-binding. Oftentimes, he would find himself browsing the shops of Armani, Clyde & Foster, and other high-end retailers. By the end of the week, his new wardrobes could be found collecting dust in some Salvation Army or other needy place. He liked to travel light.

The smoke in the tavern, as the old tube TV squawked, was thick and twisted up into plumes before the rays of fading light that trespassed through the wooded shutters. It offered no offense to his senses. He could occasionally stand a draw from a wooden pipe but it was the drinking that was his vice. And, it was drinking that the fair-skinned newswoman had been going on about.

Jesse pushed his half glass of stout toward the inside of the bar away from him and slid his chair back. He made his way closer to the TV, squeezed himself between the backs of two gentlemen at the end of the bar and leaned closer to catch the story. It would be ten minutes before he left the tavern lost in troubling thoughts.

The snow was coming now in drifts. Jesse pulled his suit-coat tight around his neck and pressed the top hat firmly down with his other hand. The Inn where he was staying wasn't far. In fact, it was so close, he could already make out the faint wisp of smoke coming from the small cluster of lodgings that surrounded it. It was perhaps a ten-minute walk from here, and though the icy wind cut deep, the time to think still made the venture enticing.

He thought of the newscast and what the implications may mean to him. He was an alcoholic, no doubt, but the bottle was often his sole companion during his many excursions. His father had been hospitalized many years earlier from a genetic anomaly—some neurodegenerative illness—which causes an accelerated form of Alzheimer's. This gene had obviously been passed on to Jesse at birth, hell, even now he forgot the most recent events unless he focused on them for a long while. This is what he was attempting now, as he made his way through the alleyways of Cricklewood, which had accumulated well over three inches of snow and ice.

The cobblestone had disappeared beneath layers of fine white silt, and the streets were eerily silent, besides the cooing sound of the drifts winding their ways around the corners of the village dwellings, which were locked up tight as if a hurricane were ensuing. He passed the familiar windows, eyes of the alleyways, and when he looked up they favored paintings cloaked behind the gentle veil of snow, the thick yellow lights pouring their reflections at Jesse's feet.

Goose pimples rode the length of Jesse's arms as he pulled the large door of the Inn out against the wind.

To be shortchanged at birth was bad enough, but now he had to deal with, *this*?! According to that lady on the television, alcohol was one of the most contributing factors of Alzheimer's disease.

'Great!,' he thought as he entered the safety of his Inn.

***

The warmth from the lodge immediately permeated his suit. The lodge he had procured for himself this week was very quaint. This narrow stone structure of two stories, despite its modern commodities, was overrun with oil lamps. There was a strapping young lad behind the counter, who always donned a beaming smile; Jesse would guess the owners' son.

Reclining quite comfortably on an easy chair across the room in the lobby was an Indian girl of middle-age; the same Indian girl who had been in this very spot night after night. He caught himself staring, mesmerized by the green splendor of her eyes, and quickly removed his top hat and coat as if to remain natural.

Shaking the moisture from his jacket, Jesse tossed it over the back of the vacant loveseat next to her and near the space heater by the coffee table. He sat to warm his hands and glanced timidly at her, trying to steal small details of her face. Her hair, though not tied up or braided in the usual fashion, was elegantly draped down her back and lined her features naturally and effortlessly. So fine was the hair from her bangs, pushed back at her ears, it merely cast a dim shadow over the flushness of her high cheekbones. Her skin was but only a shade lighter than his own, her pink lips a perfect fig.

Realizing again that he had begun to stare, he reached nervously to the bowl of crisps on the table. 'Anything to soak up some of the alcohol,' he thought to himself.

It was odd for him to sit here in the lobby after a night at the pub. If not for her and the extreme cold, he would have made his way up the stairs to his room and crumpled into a deep sleep on the mattress. But she had been there, again, and it had been cold … and she *had* him. She had him wondering where she came from and why she sat here alone, night after night, such content about her.

What he'd give for the secret of that contentment, but he would never ask her, never interfere with someone so peacefully enthralled. 'Why trouble someone so content and beautiful with my problems,' he would say to himself. But on this night, he wouldn't have to ask.

He was startled by the pressure of her hand lightly on his arm and his eyes moved to her lips, the color of a guava's flesh, and she began to speak.

"Another night, just from the tavern, eh?"

Her English accent was brilliant, an accent that Jesse, despite his travels at large, could only falsely imitate.

His American demeanor however, was obvious.

"My drinking?" he almost felt guilty.

"Your drinking. Each night you return from town I smell a different liquor on you. It simply makes me wonder."

He studied her. She would be inquiring of him, when she was so much more intriguing than he was? Not kidding himself, he exhaled with a sigh to realize that he would tell her everything if she would listen.

"Please. Something,"—there was that accent again, and her eyes so soft— "must be the culprit in it all. You know what they say about doing the same thing over and over again."

He put his hand gently on top of hers and drank in the caring expression that had become so foreign to him. He softened.

"I do. But of course, I'm not expecting a different result." he paused momentarily, wincing inside as he recounted deeply suppressed feelings. "Actually, quite the contrary."

"Well, I was raised to give that which I wish to receive. That's why I'd offer my ear. In my case, you may find that the debt outweighs the favor."

She liked him and her clever line of questioning was testing his wits.

"A trade then? Even swap. One tale for another," he said questionably, meeting her match.

At that moment, the door of the Inn was suddenly thrust open and two men—whom he recognized from the bar—stumbled in noisily grasping onto one another trying to keep themselves upright.

Immediately, the lad at the desk went to their assistance, pulling the heavy door closed behind the miscreants. As the young boy struggled at convincing the two men to allow him their coats, Jesse knew he was about to find himself in a situation.

He never should have taken the liberty to speak with this beautiful woman! What had he been thinking? Every time he got on with some hot little minx there were always the oafish, more brute-looking men, there to cause trouble for him, which he could handle well enough if not for the women being evermore antagonizing, always elevating the situation. Women loved a good fight. He had learned this. Yes, learned it well, so well it was stored among his precious stock of cherished memories that he had not yet lost.

Now the brutes were shoving at the young clerk playfully and motioning that they were perfectly capable of hanging their own coats. Meanwhile, clumps of dirty snow had found their way to the slick entryway from their garments, and the poor lad was having a time trying to brush them off the tile and onto the carpet where they would be less of a nuisance.

While the clerk was busy with a linen cloth on his knees drying the landing, one of the burly men, whose hair was cut close to his scalp—unlike his friend's full dark locks—caught Jesse's glance. Of course, he then made out Jesse's involvement with Evelyn.

Fury was building inside of Jesse as he imagined the coming confrontation. Anger so sharp, not only at those two men, but also at himself. He was angry because of the way that they were treating that boy and at the thoughtless way they were eyeing his new lady friend, without a speck of consideration for consequence. And he was also deeply angry with himself, that he never dared be so rude even when he himself was overly intoxicated.

Always Jesse was the best gentleman, even when inebriated. What confidence these pompous fools exuded, and who were they to approach with such confidence? They likely, had never held themselves to any form of standard as Jesse had. Yes, Jesse was the man here and these two were just street savages, might as well be dirty rotten thieves!

Jesse's nails dug into the palms of his hands as he looked back at the woman and wondered if they had even exchanged names.

"Jesse," she said to him, "are you coming?"

His eyes followed her finger as she pointed toward the narrow staircase where the smoke seemed to draw in on itself—must be a draft from an open room upstairs? The rectangular hole into the dark above, which was the only portal to the lofty guestrooms, reminded him of climbing into the attic of much larger estates.

Boot heels rapped upon wooden planks as they climbed, hand-in-hand.

Had this really happened? Had this woman truly saved him from an uneasy decision at the very last moment? Was he so intriguing as to deserve this? Either way, the men downstairs must have felt put out by the way she grasped his hand merrily, and with a sweet smile and a tug to his feet had beckoned him away happily as if 'he' were her choice and not them! And so, the trouble would be postponed—for now.

II

Evelyn

Obviously, Evelyn knew which room he had been staying in; it took no effort for her to pick it out among the twelve rooms, which occupied the upstairs of the Brunswick Inn.

She waited patiently, admiring again the deep hues of purple and red that rode the length of the hallway carpet, as Jesse removed the key from his left coat pocket and pressed it firmly into the bronze chamber of the door. The flame in the sconce adorning the entryway pulled heavily as the draft from the door caught it closing behind them.

His room was uniform with the rest of the lodge's, making it familiar and easy for Evelyn to find her way past the thick, red-pinstriped bed to pull out one of the small chairs about the round coffee table. Jesse had somehow remembered his coat among the excitement downstairs and for now it rested on the bed. Now, here he was, settled into his own chair across from one of the most witty and intriguing women he had ever met. He found himself watching her every move, even the simplest of things. The way her thumb ran its way along the edge of the round glass table, as if smoothing supple clay, captured him more and more.

"Can you hear them giggling?" Evelyn asked softly, then continued, "The three girls down the hall? Weeks now ... laughing. Wonder what they're up to in there?"

Jesse sensed sarcasm at the raise of her brow. He hears the familiar faint laughter and seeing the crystal tumbler sitting in the sill of the window, made a slow move to push himself back up out of his seat hoping to soften his subtle judgment of their lesbian affairs.

"How could I not," he said, his hand firm on the small back of mahogany. "Scotch?"

He is now standing firmly upright and she has caught sight of the solitary tumbler as well, "You only have one glass, Jesse. What will you drink?"

Jesse made the two paces to the sill as he waved absently. Picking up the glass and sliding it onto the small countertop alcove, he reached beneath where an ice bucket always awaited his return.

"We'll just have to share," he smiled sideways, "No, as you've not failed to notice, I have had quite my fill tonight."

As the cubes of ice hit the bottom of the glass, his intentions are provided him and she accepts.

Jesse had pulled a lavish bottle of Johnnie Walker from the dark of the miniature bedside kitchenette. The liquor moved and cracked the ice within the crystal as he poured, composing a jingling sound, which reminded Evelyn of the Christmas snows that her father would tell tales about late into the night. It seemed funny that upon this night the same snows were falling in early October. She watched as he swirled the fine liquor in the glass and then placed it on the table in front of her. Her hand out, she motioned for him to reclaim his seat.

"Those girls intrigue me—" her hand drops to the rim of the glass.

"You?!" he had tactfully interjected, "Let me assure you they are quite 'intriguing' to me as well."

Her finger ran along the smooth edge of the crystal and she grasped it intimately in her hand. Jesse noticed that her skin tone was not far from the tone of the tonic itself. She paused before she sipped, "Are you jealous of them?"

He met her gaze and noticed the sides of her mouth curling into a mischievous sneer. "Hardly! Well, not nearly as you!"

Evelyn lowered her drink halfway to the table in a stunned motion, "Am not!" Then lifting it back said, "Well, maybe a little."

They smiled together, and he felt the crimson-flush in his own cheeks rise.

Soon they were both sitting comfortably as if they had known one another for years. On through the night they exchanged observation after observation about their quaint little hotel. Jesse filled Evelyn's glass twice with the expensive Scotch, as he told her about his disorder and the disturbing news he heard in the bar. Evelyn, in turn, told him of her father's Christmas stories of which the ice had so reminded her.

"But there is still something I don't understand, Evelyn"—now perhaps he could seize the opportunity to dig deeper—"I see you night after night in the lobby, and never out on the streets. So what did you come here, to this place for, if not for only a comfortable perch to enjoy your people watching?"

A corner-mouthed smirk was followed by her nostalgic gaze, as if she were stretching out a mental hand to the past. The sullen look told Jesse that it was painful to remember.

"It was nearly thirteen years ago that I left the Oxychana Tribe against my parents' wishes. I had been closely watched my entire life up to that point. My father was a very powerful man; he had traveled extensively and filled my head with all the stories that a girl would ever dream. In the end, I think it was these stories that would fuel the engine of my desire, which helped me to make the choice and leave ..."

Jesse saw the soft light in her eyes pull back, as if she was digging deep back into her past and captured the moment to express his empathy, "So you wanted more, but why did they fight you on leaving?"

She could still recall the sandy floors of their adobe home, which had been dug into the side of a jagged mound of clay. The fires that littered the town at night still shone in her mind, the wisps of smoke and the sound of the whip-poor-wills cooing that moved within their oh-so-hidden community. The canopy of the rainforest parted high overhead allowing the sun to dry the Earth during the day, where mother was a master gardener. She remembered watching, as her mom would turn the soil along the moist edge of the forest, because that was where the best peppers would grow. The outskirts of her village were alive with colors year-round. Vegetables and fruits of every variety formed a sanctuary for the villagers there. They loved to be among the harvest whether working or not.

"It was a reap and sow existence, give and get. 'As the Earth does for us, we do for the Earth', Father used to say..." then nostalgically, "we are truly one.

"Understand, Jesse, I had been brought up as a Seeker. Schooled not only by my father and his stories, but by my mother, whose magic was sought out by the most elite for her knowledge and medicines.

"Our tribe, Oxychana, derived its name from the herb my mother utilized in her metaphysical states. We developed Quids out of a type of Sage which had been discovered ages ago. Its petals so blue, but the power was in the root. The elders would roll up the ground herbs in the leaf, then pack the Quids between their gums and teeth. The juices would render vivid visions of their ancestors and other spirits of the Earth.

"My mother was Chieftain when it came to it. We practiced together in my youth. And so," she tilted the glass as to see the small amount of scotch remaining within, "it grew ingrained in me."

Reminiscently and matter-of-factly she lifted the glass to her cheek fully aware of how ridiculous she must sound, “I was fated to marry the man of the Sun and bring harmony to our tribe, which had already begun to fall victim to segregation in the onrush of modern age.” She tossed back the remainder of the glass.

“Can we not perhaps move back down to the lobby?” she asked. “I have a sudden urge for a smoke.”

“Absolutely.”

Jesse regained his composure. He had been listening to her story and found it enthralling, while wondering how she had managed that pure and perfect skin throughout such a primitive upbringing.

Evelyn reached out to brace herself on the small table to stand, but Jesse captured her hand in mid-reach.

“Unsure of your own balance, now are we?” With a chuckle, he helped her to her feet.

She quickly regained composure and sauntered her way to the door.

“I’ll be right down,” Jesse said as he doubled back to the bedside kitchenette to fetch his wooden pipe. ‘Just such an occasion,’ he thought to himself with a smile.

The first few steps down to the lobby brought back thoughts of the jackals that had been causing trouble with the clerk, but it had been a long while since then, and there were no signs of the two. Instead, Evelyn waited patiently, lounging on the sofa with her white cigarette held casually between her first and second fingers, elbow propped upon the arm of the couch and her legs crossed. The side of her long skirt had a hemmed slit up its length, revealing her caramel smooth skin up to the thigh.

The owner, Gerald, now stood behind the counter. A man of sixty years, well-dressed, and an avid pipe-smoker. Jesse took advantage of this fact, and before sitting closely to Evelyn this time, stopped and asked for a pinch of that cherry tobacco he could faintly smell drifting through the air.

Striking a match to light his pipe brought with the flame that familiar glimmer of blue to Evelyn’s attention.

“You have gorgeous eyes,” she said, looking into them as she blew smoke in a thin line up to the ceiling, and then leaned back to relax. “I don’t think I have ever seen a shade of blue like that in a dark-skinned man.”

He considered what she had said for a moment and then told her that it’s his father’s eyes that he carries. He glanced down at her legs and the shade of color in them and reveled in the way she has called him ‘dark-skinned’. No one had called him that in a considerable while, though likely due to his prosperity, he always believed his skin tone was just light enough that no one would dare, for fear of being called foolish. He thought back for a moment of his father.

He thought of his father’s eyes and the way he always got lost in them.

“My father’s eyes were the only way I ever really got a sense of who he was. I never knew my mother. Pops could never remember enough to know for sure who she was, or who she’d been. By the time I was old enough to start visiting him at the retirement home, memories of her had completely disappeared.” He settled back remembering, “I started into my trust fund at eighteen and began visiting my father on a weekly basis. Really I’m ashamed to admit it, but I kept it up as a moral obligation for my trust and all. I just couldn’t see the point when he wasn’t himself anymore. I still feel like a brat for being left my trust.

"I mean, I would sit, and mostly listen as he rambled about various pieces of his past, but most of it sounded more like a fairytale than reality. As far as his life, it’s a puzzle to me. He remembered me for the most part, until they moved him to the hospital one day. I couldn’t bear seeing him like that. His memory was severely warped, and I couldn’t help but see my possible likely fate in him. So I left America, haven’t gone back since. That was five years ago.”

Evelyn was watching him intently, this man in fine clothing, spilling out the pain of his past to her, revealing a side of himself that reminded her of her own heartaches. The white shirt that had been unbuttoned at the collar and at the cuffs brought to life the beautiful blend of culture in his face. 'His heritage is perhaps richer than mine is,' she thought to herself as she visually traced the bone around each eye, the sculpted jaw leading to the cleft chin. Compelling cheeks that allowed color to show his emotion were not too darkened by the sun.

He turned his head to her, "So you were telling me of these Quids?" His interest was genuine; she could see it in his demeanor. "You say they could help you see the future?"

She laughed, and flicked the ash of her cigarette behind her, "If that were so, The Fae would have showed me here long ago!" She waved her cigarette around and made a strong gesture toward Jesse, "Which, is precisely *why* I am here! How can I know if what occurred under the influence of Oxychana has any natural meaning for me? There was so much truth behind my mother's teachings—walking in hand with the Maiden, Mother and Crone—but it was dad bringing home tales from a distance that made me start rethinking myself.

"I loved the feeling of water through my toes and fingers as I searched for special little stones. Among the physical beauty of the flowing streams and scent of the leaves I felt as if I'd brought the world of the Fae to life, rather than just dreamed of them. I loved to go off with Serat into the jungle and climb into the canopy far from the village. But those things got harder to do as I smoked Oxychana, and my mother became more protective of me. The older I got, the closer I became with the Fae," her eyes demanded Jesse's attention from under her lashes, "they were inhabitants of the spirit world; their glamour and allure always intoxicating. The more I flew, the more disconnected I felt from the waking world."

Through the drifting smoke, her cloudy eyes told Jesse that she was judging the behaviors of her past. "I was fourteen when my father started sending the suitors to me. One a month, sometimes two, but mother would turn them all away, making each one journey into trance with her before she would ever decide. It went on and on; my father traveling, my mother trancing. I, on the other hand, spent my time, keeping a clear head again—a fact the Fae did not particularly like—sneaking out and speaking with the villagers, escaping into the jungle in the early morning with my friends and dreaming of seeing the tops of steel structures and automobiles!" Her eyes had widened as she spoke, and the word automobiles sounded so funny in proper English.

"Your accent," Jesse couldn't get past it, "I'd have guessed you were born here."

Evelyn smiled, and for the first time he sensed a bit of shyness in her. She took a slow deep drag from her cigarette, nearly offing the last half in one big ash.

Setting the remainder in the copper foil tray on the end table she said, “Well, where do you think I’ve been the last many years? And, in a way you could say my people had an origin that begun in Europe. The Oxychana are fabled to be a surviving link to the Anglo-Saxon lineage of those commanded by Bran the Blessed.”

“You’re kidding. I know the name.” said he.

“But did you know he advised the pagans to flee underground during the Roman Catholic uprising?”

“It’s the very reason I am here! Anglesley, Avalon, and the church’s attempt at eradicating the Druids and Priestesses.”

“Such were my descendants, so it goes. It’s been so long since I’ve thought of such things."

Jesse cupped the wooden pipe between his palms and propped his elbows upon his knees, "It’s as if I have been studying your lineage. There's not much I like more than deep history, especially the legends. I’m determined to see Wales and the Isle of the Dragon."

He felt much more sober now and was attempting to make sense of her supposed heritage and colorful story, "We are not even remotely close to your West African homeland so how is such a distant connection possible?"

She took only as much offense to this question as Jesse would have to the contrasting color of his eyes and ethnicity. She gave him the benefit of the doubt, "I can really only tell you what I have read in the leaves. Legends, as you call them, likely begin with some simple truth, don't you think?"

"Of course. I wouldn't be here today, were I not trying to convince myself that fairytales are rooted in history. One of the reasons I want to see the Isle of Wight is just to row out to the Needles and see for myself if a dragon’s skeleton really lies there."

Evelyn relaxed a little when Jesse made this statement. A reaction to her underlying giddiness at such remarkable conversation.

She said, "Maybe this is the common denominator between us. Travel brought me here in a small effort to perhaps discover some remnant of the subterranean tunnels that were said to have run beneath the entirety of the continent. I read, within our leave houses, that it was by those tunnels that our people found their new sanctuary."

Jesse's interest piqued. "Leaves, you say? You would scry"—and then seeing that she had trouble understanding—"look into leaves for answers?"

"I think we're getting carried away in myth. The leaves were just our way of passing down stories without violating our laws of writ. Though such laws have long been impossible to implement, our leaf houses still stand, and can be read by but a few. The leaves were like our history books strung out on long lines and marked with Ogham letters."

"Like the leaves of a book?" Jesse interjected.

"Yes. exactly," a nod to the curious but relevant observation. It was something she had not thought of before, "The Ogham alphabet that's written on the leaves is one of the most telling remnants of our line. Sometimes I wish such things would either burn or reveal their ancient truths to stop the damaging arguments that result. My mother and Serat, my old guardian, had so much faith in my position. It was a religious passion that scared me, and in some ways, still does. That's why I couldn't rightly go back to my parents after … well, after he left me."

"He? Who is he?"

For the first time, Jesse spied the pale skin on her ring finger. It reminded him of scar tissue, this being a remnant of the 'he' she now spoke of, no doubt.

Evelyn saw his eyes fixed on it and reached with her right hand to touch the very place, "The war.

"It was getting late one afternoon, we were out in the jungle, Serat and I, hunting the monstrous explosions we'd been hearing for weeks. The village was a bit too far to be bothered by them, and Serat was the only one brave enough to dare go so close as earshot with me.

"It was the first time I laid eyes on him, my Adam. A man of white skin as I had never seen. My English was broken at best, but his French was very good.

"His left leg was hurt, obviously hit by something, for he braced himself against a Wattle Tree and limped. His eyes were blue like yours. I could see them as he winced each movement. Serat was holding me back with his strong arm but I was being adamant with him. As soon as I had caught sight of him through the fronds, no one could've stopped me from knowing him."

"Where was he from? A white man in Africa, and when did you say this was—back in the sixties?" Jesse questioned her, not morally, but rather inquisitively.

"1968 during the Biafran African War. He had gone the opposite direction after being wounded and was resting after realizing he must backtrack through enemy fire. I pleaded with Serat to let me tend to him and he finally gave way, staying close by me while I spoke to Adam. I knew my mother could heal him, but there was no way Serat was going to let me bring a foreign man-of-war back to our village, or anywhere near it. So I begged for him to go and fetch her while I kept an eye on Adam."

"Wow. That's amazing. So war was waging only miles away from where your village was?" Jesse asked, shaking his head.

"Oh, yes. And it wasn't the only war going on at the time. There was war everywhere. Being a remote people like we were was our safety net, at times. The Civil War was also raging in Nigeria. In my own little part of Africa it was all just another exciting time for me. Anytime Serat and I would come across trenches, left behind by dozers, it just made me more curious." That look of widened eyes and mischief again befell her.

Jesse pulled on the pipe sizzling the cherry scent, and when the pipe came away, the smoke formed a perfect thick ring in the air. "So what happened? Did Serat go to fetch your mother?"

"He did."

Evelyn now took on a worried look as she spoke, "He left swiftly, but when he returned with her, I was gone. Were it not for Adam's urgency, and my need for adventure, I might have stayed. You must understand, he had no intent on coming back to my village, *or* to remain put. He only needed someone to help him.

"As I spoke with him, he surely sensed my willingness to go with him, away from where I had come. And so he asked me. It wouldn't take a single moment for me to decide. Before I knew it, I had his arm over my shoulder and I was pushing through the forest toward his base where he assured me medical attention awaited."

She looked to Jesse as if she were caught in a dream. The smell of the cherry smoke had livened her senses and brought her back to the cabin with Adam. The fine wood tables, the cherry trees blossoming in the yard, and their own piece of land on the base of Colonel Murtala Mohammed.

She recounted the way he would make her laugh, as he read from the Bible and commented on her English, "Adam funded the Christian missionaries from France. He had moved into Nigeria before the war had begun and after accepting Colonel Mohammed's generosity for so long, he found himself fighting alongside him for civil rights."

The loneliness in Evelyn's gaze was piercing now as she watched Jesse take another drag of the pungent tobacco. He couldn't bear the sight of her lips turning down so unnaturally and her eyes fixed perfectly to one spot, unanimated, unlike her. His loneliness too, was inwardly apparent to him, but he would not show it physically. He briefly moved to offer her some of his pipe but was taken aback, when she shook her head silently.

"Me too," he said, commenting on her look of exhaustion.

Some life entered her again and she leaned forward reaching down to the hem of her skirt and pulled it taut over her upper thigh, which had become evermore exposed throughout their conversation.

"I am sorry, the Scotch has taken quite a toll on me tonight and it is getting close to dawn, now. It's rare to find such genuine conversation."

Jesse pushed himself up from the sofa, capped his pipe and slid it into the back pocket of his slacks.

He turned to Evelyn, who was eyeing him oddly, and as he bowed to her said, "Agreed. A conversation worth remembering."

Her expression lightened again as she took his hand gingerly.

Jesse began to tug her to her feet, "Although I could sit forever listening to your voice, I must be the gentleman and accompany you to your door until another day."

Feeling herself pulled upright to him, now very close, she could smell the sweet cherry on his breath while his free hand assisted the contour of her hip.

"I trust your room is upstairs. You wouldn't be sleeping here in the lobby where I found you, I suppose? Though it *is* the most familiar setting."

His playful remark transformed her weary expression into a beaming smile, "Room seven, at the end of the hall."

Taking the flight of stairs proved a bit more challenging to them both now, but they did so hand-in-hand. The lighted sconces had long since gone out and the ceiling cast an orange glow, with the coming sunrise filtering through the beveled glass of one solitary window pane.

As they reached the top, he pulled her arm over his shoulder, "Now I can know how it must have felt for you, helping Adam back to base! I am only thankful that *you* do not require medical attention at this point."

Evelyn pushed him away playfully, and their shoulders came back together as they made their way toward the end of the corridor to her room.

He watched as she, more than obviously, reached into her bosom with a shy, "Oh!" and removed her key. As she began working the lock, the door of the room behind them burst open.

A young girl, clad in nothing more than a nightgown, tugged her friend into the hallway when they were stopped short in play by the sight of Jesse and Evelyn. The smell of patchouli emanated from both of the giddy blondes. Evelyn turned her head and saw the petite gal in striped shorts and a cut tee shirt, peer over her friend's shoulder to get sight of what was going on. Both young girls looked as if they had just walked in on someone doing something they weren't supposed to see.

"Ladies," Jesse gestured, with an arm extended to the lobby.

The roommates looked at one another and giggled as they backed into their room and shut the door.

Evelyn turned slowly up to meet Jesse's eyes and both laughed heartily.

"It looks like it's going to be a long night," Evelyn said, as she finally freed the lock and stepped into the crack of her doorway.

Jesse stood with his left hand in his pocket and his right thumb inside the lapel of his white shirt. He offered a simple nod and with utmost confidence said, "Until tomorrow then, miss?"

His steel blue eyes melted her insides again. Still, she nodded.

"Until tomorrow."

The door closed with a quiet click, and Jesse's back was already turned as he headed to his room.

III

Room Six

The three young women stood around an oval wooden end table in room six of the Brunswick Inn. The furniture of this room had been moved around in a particular fashion that allowed more space for dance and play. The oaken bed had been placed against the picture window, which always stayed pulled tight. Three small candles and the light from an unusual cup brought the interior of the room to life.

The cup, a large chalice made from the mother-of-pearl they had brought from the base of Snowdonia Mountain rested on the oval slab between them and images in the chalice swirled as the three spoke amongst themselves.

Veronica, the eldest, was thirty-two, but her cheeks, the color of cherry blossoms, showed no sign of age. Her voice alone was distinguished while the trio was as one, for it flowed always in rhyme with her eyes shut tight.

"She is ripe as a melon turned twice. Tonight is the night to pluck the grape from the vine, for in time the fruit of her womb will bring a child to the seat of power, a child of the old blood line."

Emily was stirring the nectar in the chalice with a pink fingernail as her perfect smile beamed beneath twenty-year-old blue eyes, ringed with perfect purple eyeliner. Her voice was distinguishable by the constant rhythm in her speech as her eyes maintained a half-lidded flutter.

"Too long have we been away—the crow's feet tug at Jessica—her eyes show signs of age—we will waste away outside the Fae," giggling in Jessica's direction and sneering, she silenced herself before offering any further insult.

Jessica was twenty-nine, but had spent the least amount of time in the spirit world. For this, she was constantly ridiculed. She showed more years than the other two, for they lived mostly in the world of the Fae, and it was a well-known fact that time passed much slower in the otherworld. When Jessica spoke, her eyes were wide-open and the words came always with reason.

"The veil is a constant cloud to your judgment here, in this place. Your allure is your strength, but it is clear to me alone that already the Mother's will has been set adrift on the sea of potential. As we speak the two think of one another—their thoughts like fingers of energy—out across the hall they reach, and what mingles in the middle is a powerful bonding urge."

Emily winced at this as if she had been dealt an insult of her own, but cackled wildly in response.

The Mother had taught them well that nothing could hold power to hurt them if they learned to laugh at it.

Emily lifted her dripping nail to her lips and sucked the nectar from it before pressing the issue further, “You speak as if we are here only to witness that the Will be done. The power of the Fae is great, and standing idly by will not do for me at all.”

With that, Veronica raised a hand gently in a gesture of silence and immediately earned the two girls’ reverence, “Sister is correct. The ship is adrift, fingers of desire are tip-to-tip. But to bring forth an unborn takes desire of three, our thoughtful presence multiplies this feat.”

Jessica reasoned to Emily, “There must be the desire of the Mother, the Father, *and* the forthcoming child, to become one, before conception will occur. The Holy Trinity must be present for the magic to commence. In this way, it is ultimately the child’s desire that we must await. We can only amplify this desire by mingling our thoughts into those of this union. The Mother’s will, portrayed through our three thoughts, will yield our preference when the unborn joins in the desire to become one on this plane. Witness, yes, but be mindful, we must, of the fruits of her womb.”

Understanding is audibly exchanged throughout room six in the form of laughter and joined hands. Circling the shell chalice in dance, they gaze upon the manifesting face of the Mother within.

IV

Ecstasy

Giggling emanated from room six again.

Lying there beside his coat, which lay on top of the bedspread, Jesse heard clearly now these girls whose giggling had plagued his nights here. Staring at the ceiling he wondered if Evelyn heard it, too. She surely did, her room being right across the hall.

As he lay there, he thought of her question, "Are you jealous?"

Rolling over to one side, he clutched firmer a pillow. 'I am tonight,' he thought. And as a subtle reminder, he spotted the tumbler on the table, sitting perfectly where she had left it, a smudge from her tender lips occupying the rim.

More giggling, passionately this time, floated through the thin walls of the establishment. Jesse couldn't help but imagine those girls making love not four rooms from his very spot. Grabbing up the neck of his coat he turned quickly off of the side of the bed, meaning to throw it over the back of the mahogany chair.

"Damn it!" he exclaims.

He knows he is to take a glass of the Scotch. His ivory fingernails are prominent as he lifts the glass, but it is not these that he is eyeing. God, no! It's the smudge. Imagining the sweet taste of Evelyn's pink lips on his, and now holding the glass between both hands, he slumps back to sit on the bed in thought, his mind busy with what ifs.

It was only as he moved to put the glass back onto the table, in a single act of determined will, that he heard the soft rapping on his door. 'It's too early for the help,' he thought, as he turned toward the noise. Then it became clear.

Pulse quickening in an instant, he pulled the door open gently and dared a look in the hope his thoughts have been heard through brick and mortar.

"I heard the giggling," she said.

Her face was serene; her hair styled straight as the finest black silk.

His body eagerly enjoyed an immediate flush; heat ran the surface of his skin. The magnetism of the moment—it is felt between them. Her feminine silhouette shown through the sheer slip of faded pink material. Her head was bowed and her hands intertwined, as if shamefully.

"I couldn't help it. I was thinking ... asking myself if I—"

And as her eyes slowly rose to meet his, Jesse seized her gaze solidly and finished her sentence, "—were jealous?"

She bashfully nodded and dropped her glance before looking back up at him through her eyelashes.

"Yes," she replied.

Immediately, Jesse captured her, pulling the door open and drawing her close to him in a crash of desire. The door closed and he was with her, turning her toward the bed as her hands made their way to his face and she lavishly claimed his mouth. Gently biting his lower lip, he maneuvered her left hand to his belt. Gliding his own left hand over the smooth fabric of her slip, he found it a simple thing to feel the contour of her hardened nipple and grope her breast feverishly, aching for his mouth to suckle it.

As his hand moved up her thigh and took the thin white cloth of her panties to slide them down, her opposite knee came up, and she wrapped her leg around him. Evelyn tugged at his buckle with one hand, and her other hand untucked his white shirt, which was now smeared with make-up. Jesse impatiently helped remove the offensive garment—pulling at it—shaking it off one arm. Passions running high, the couple hit the bed furiously.

In his thirst for her, Jesse grabbed at the buckle himself, pulled it hard in one swift jerk, then dealt with the simple clasp of his suit pants. Kicking his slacks to the ground, he took her left leg from around his back and seized the panties again, hiking the slip up ... revealing her soft butterscotch tummy ... and the sloping lines of her inner thighs.

The sweet lips of her sex urging him to her, he pulled the lace lingerie from her legs. Evelyn grasped the muscles of his arms and stretched her neck up to see him in such passion as his lips delved into the hot nectar of her love. The whole of her body pulsing, her fingers ran sensuously up his neck into his hair and around his head, pulling him deeper and tighter onto her, as his tongue explored the depths of her heat ... her inner beauty.

Clutching the trim of his shorts, she tugged him hard, beckoning him to her. Turning sideways on the bed, her hand ventured from that trim and up into the middle of his heated bulge. Feeling the strength of his muscle, Evelyn grabbed it eagerly. Uttering deep moans, he rose from his lavish playground and allowed her to yank the top of his shorts down and over her new possession, revealing it to her. Reaching with her other hand, she squeezed it, then grasped his elbow, pulling it to her, pulling *him* to her. He had pushed the slip up over her naked breasts and found her rosebud nipple with his tongue, before giving in to her and meeting her lips in a sweet, tight vise with his own.

Jesse moved into her, steadying himself with his fingers—gripping the flesh of her soft ass—clutching the pillows he has grown used to. Evelyn's hand was between their bodies, sliding around his shaft and experiencing the mingling of their skin, their exchanges of fluids. Now he was thrusting and moaning as she joined him in an age-old rhythm, seeking a completion only they could know.

Her eager body-spasm signaled her joy as her hand came away and traveled his back. Then, in a fury of passion, Evelyn sank her nails into his shoulders and her loins poured forth in a rush. Her eyes were clenched as her head rolled back and her back arched in ecstasy. In this moment, she felt the pulse of his organ and then the heat of his orgasm upon her as their desire was gratified. They tightly coiled together in the silent stillness of love.

***

The giggling had stopped. It had been replaced by the sound of Evelyn's shallow breathing. The sheets were tucked under his arm yet pulled up over her shoulders. She lay near to him dozing. His eyes trained on her peaceful expression in an effort to more solidify the memory into his faulty conscience. The tumbler still lay empty on the table; as he closed his eyes in the early morning light and he wondered what she dreamed.

V

Evelyn Dreams

Nigeria 1968

Evelyn's heart was pounding rapidly as she trudged through the damp air pulling down hard on Adam's hand. The rain had started and her knees ached under her soaked kanga from stumbling so much of the way. Adam frequently pulled her down low behind some fronds when gunfire pierced the air, stilling the curious sounds of the wilderness. It was like a devil's cry to Evelyn, but she held fast to him and allowed him to take in the whole sight of her.

Her face, so prominent against the moist leaves of the emerald forest, was soothing to his pain. The colorful garb, now riddled with mud had matted to her body making her unmistakably different, but in no way uncivilized. How becoming was the wrap she had around herself, which was originally rolled tightly at her chest. Normally loose, it now clung form-fitting to her lovely figure.

Adam sat with his back to a twisted, old, fallen tree, now decaying and host to a family of fern growth. Sliding up the tree and cocking his head back, he looked into the undergrowth ahead of them for movement. The pop of rifle rounds had grown close, two maybe three at most. Pulling a large knife from its sheath on his belt, Adam pressed it firmly into her hand.

"Just in case," he phrased the statement in French, so she understood.

"In case?" she asked him as she looked into his eyes, which now showed worry for the first time.

"If they take me. They won't shoot you—not a woman—but they may get close enough, and you may have to …" Her look tells him she understands.

Just then a commotion alarmed them in time to make out a yellowish shape beyond some prayer plants only yards away. The leaves shuffled violently and the leaf litter scattered as Evelyn gasped. Adam moved to swing the rifle from around his back, when a flurry of red feathers was joined by the horrible sound of a jungle cat's screams.

The jaguar pounced and was upon the bird, leaping off into the trees, before Adam had completely readied his defense. Both of them had held their breath, but now enjoyed a sigh of relief as they met each other's gaze. Wide-eyed, Evelyn met his grin and shook her head in a universal sign of synicism

The brush was a gnarly mass, and the rain was breaking through the canopy in waterfalls. But Adam seemed to have regained some of his strength, and they moved low and quickly now, always behind where their cover was thickest. They had covered miles and the dark was threatening to be upon them any moment. Palmettos hacked off at the base had been their only guide and here they were surrounded by them.

"We're close," he whispered, pointing through the night at what seemed like a void carved into the forest wall. "We should be just a few clicks from the border, but there's hardly any cover beyond the breach of the forest."

She looked at him questioningly, "But, we have seen no one."

Adam glanced in her direction with a finger to his lips, "They're out there. The problem is nobody knows we are coming. I'll have to alarm them. Stay here, and be ready."

She watched as he moved away, barely letting his limp impede his movement.

'He is a man of strength in the large world,' she thought to herself, 'a man without fear.'

The long golden locks, which were now darkened by the weather, were a rare thing for her to behold in the jungle. Only during rare occasions from outside upon visitors or her suitors did she see such color. And even then, it was unnatural for their skin. Adam's hair complimented him consummately and she could envision it well-washed and tended. He had slung his rifle back over his shoulder and gone beyond the giant elephant ear leaves, which acted like gutters to the downfall of water from above. He disappeared, his camouflage hiding him well from prying eyes.

She became aware of the jungle's liveliness again, as the dark enveloped and her eyes grew accustomed. Sounds of various creatures, the native birds and insect varieties, took on a blanket effect in the night. She didn't like this loneliness, here on the edge of a jungle she once thought of as impenetrable, here on the cusp of everything her father had filled her head with over the years, *here*— on the brink of change.

A piercing whistle mightier than any eagle call sliced through the night air over the sounds of the rain, and Adam burst from the leaves reaching for her arm with an eagerness that made her forget his injuries. He tugged her to her feet and started toward the darkness of the open air where she now saw a light in the distance too high to be natural.

"Go now!" barked Adam, as gunfire paraded from the forest not five hundred yards from where they emerged.

It was then that she saw the silver and gold lights coming from the jungle in a steady stream toward the sky. Her mind had no time to recount the New Year's fire her father spoke of from his travels to Asia, but it was the same. She would not let go of Adam. And though he had turned his back to her with his rifle aimed into the denseness from where they'd come, she clutched even tighter pulling him along. The piercing wail of the rocket was blurring her train of thought but she vaguely made out structures in the dark, and before long saw the twists of wire with spiked barbs coiled around wood.

"I see something!" she managed to say among the noise, not knowing if he heard, or if he cared.

Gunshots, from behind, rang out one after another, and the ground sprang to life around them. Leaf and mud spattered in unison with each shot, some bullets leaving trails through the wet terrain like whips in action. She thought of dropping but kept running until Adam's rifle came to life with a devastating sound she had never heard so close. She stumbled in the wet mud, forcing him down to one knee, as she clasped her ears. Adam let loose three consecutive shots before yanking her up and pushing her forward, urging her to continue. She could make out the shape of soldiers in the distance moving closer, and as she squinted in the torrential downfall of rain to make things clearer, an explosion rocked the earth not a hundred feet distant, sending mud pelting them as they ran!

Adam was screaming in French, "I'm here! Fire! Fire!"

The horizon lit up with an array of gunshot, brilliant enough to illuminate the source of the constant drumming she had been hearing. There stood an awning of metal, built quite poorly, but finally making a distinct welcome entrance into where they were headed.

Another explosion nearer the forest—orginating from this side—cast the couple's dark shadows ahead, wreathed in orange hue.

As they entered, happy to be secure from the wet and metal rain … steady drumming on the roof remained.

***

It seemed ages before they were finally at rest in the infirmary. The men had helped Adam onto a small Rover amidst heated arguments, which had been obvious to Evelyn related to her. Yet, Adam had always persevered and kept her by his side. Assuring her it would all be okay, and comforting her through every mishap.

Adam explained quietly what she was seeing for the first time in her life. Though the storm was thundering all around, she was wide-eyed at the extraordinary sights she beheld. The vehicle they had traveled in at uneasy speeds, the light she had seen from the darkness, which had emanated from a tower of smooth rock, sealed tightly with glass; the water was sent streaming down instead of being let into the establishment.

The building they were now in was even more intriguing. The floors were made of fine white tiles, with partially reflective surfaces. Beds of smooth, clean cotton, and soft pillows were held off the ground on steel metal frames with wheels, allowing them to glide freely from place to place. Trinkets of all types occupied the shelves, and drawers of a sturdy cream material, called plastic, housed a variety of useful medical tools, which they used as they tended to Adam while she watched.

The place's smell made her uneasy at first, but she knew they were safe here. Never had she seen a place so uniform, so entirely closed in, yet so massive. Everywhere she looked was clean, white, and new; a completely different world from the humid outside where the rains had begun to calm. If she hadn't just come through the foreboding forest and into this white haven, illuminated by soft electrical lights, she may never know it was dark outside right now. Only the small square portholes that gave view to outside were the bit of evidence as to the time of day.

Lovely women in pure white attended him, and one took Evelyn by the hand and led her to a small room with polished metal fixtures. The woman explained to Evelyn that they ran water and that she could bathe. A fresh change of clothes and a towel were left on the counter for her. Evelyn looked into the mirror above the sink and saw herself as she would often be found as a child, covered in filth from head to toe and her hair in disarray.

'Oh, what mother would say to me now?' she thought to herself, as she untwisted the fabric of her kanga and began peeling the mud-stiffened material from her body. She turned the knob in the shower and smiled. Steam began to rise, and she put her hand first into the wonderful jet before joyfully immersing herself in it. The water cascaded down in thin streams over her slim figure.

Evelyn had taken a whole twenty minutes in the washroom, but had managed to brush her teeth and pull the knots from her hair with her fingers. When she emerged she saw Adam sitting upright and speaking to a very tall, dark-bearded man in pressed camouflage. The man was decorated with gold pendants and striped with colored material. He was gesturing to Adam to take the keys from his hand, when Adam's eyes fell upon her.

The gown she adorned was but a simple white thing, with buttons up the chest to the collar, which she had failed to fasten. But her skin was so beautiful. Her green eyes were piercing. And the way the corners of her mouth turned naturally up upon his glance made his gaze all too noticeable to his visitor.

"Evelyn!" Adam said, taking the keys from the man. "Colonel, here she is now."

He winced and braced himself on the metal framework as he got to his feet, secretly waving her to come near.

Approaching the Colonel she realized how tall the man really was, inches taller than Adam and a good foot above her. The man's eyes were yellowed but still wide, not weary in the least.

'Another great man of power,' she thought to herself.

The gentleman reached slowly and took her hand. Gingerly lifting it before him he said, "I am indebted to *you*, miss. You must be exhausted from lugging our Adam home." He turned his head to Adam and made a gesture, which was hard for her to see. "You are quite brave."

Evelyn bowed her head to him, unsure of what to say as Adam's comment saved her.

"Yes. Evelyn, this is Colonel Mohammed. He has agreed to let you stay here, with me. If it would be comfortable for you, I have quite a lodge not far from here; there is plenty of room. Of course, if you would like to go back ..."

Her soul sank for a moment at the thought, and she was adamant when she spoke, "No." Then fearing her urgency may have betrayed her, "At least not until your wounds are healed, that is."

Finding tempo again she asked, "You will not be going back into battle immediately, will you Adam?"

With this the Colonel laughed and patted her hand, "Just as I said, a strong woman. Were it up to her, she would have you back there this coming morning."

Laughing, he let her hand fall, "I can see you have much to learn, and Adam will have plenty of time to show you around. Our home is yours for as long as you'd like."

Mohammed turned to Adam and put a strong hand on his shoulder, "I'm glad you're back, my friend. Get some rest. God bless."

He tipped the camouflage covering on his head in ceremonious gesture, on his way to the door, "My lady."

"I feel bad being so comfortable and you've not yet bathed." Evelyn said to Adam.

Though his wound had been cleaned and sutured, then wrapped in gauze, the rest of him was still covered in filth. His left pant leg had been simply torn away in order to work with his injuries.

"Don't. I would much rather be home where I have a fresh change of clothes and my very own shower."

He reached over to the bedside counter and grabbed a black leather-bound book with golden pages, "God's will in due time," Then holding it aloft before folding it to his chest, "My bible. Mohammed brought it to me."

Noticing she didn't quite understand, Adam immediately had an urge to help her find her place. All cleaned up, he could tell she was young, perhaps seventeen. He took the crutch beside the bed in his left hand, and tucked it under his armpit, when an idea formed.

With an extremely mischievous grin he looked to her and said, "Wanna drive a car?"

VI

Tragedy

Adam and Evelyn were inseparable, like two peas in a pod. Besides the occasional run to the annex for snacks, they were never apart.

It had been more than six months since she had found Adam in the jungle and, since that time, had soaked up much knowledge about the present era. The stories Adam would tell her, and the pictures he would show her, overshadowed her father's tales, and eventually smoothed the memory of them from the forefront of her mind. Adam was easily thirty-years-old, but from the time he stepped out of the washroom, after coming from the jungle, she was captivated by him. His hair so sheen, golden like the center point of a daisy, his eyes like cobalt stone.

She would wrap his leg for him each night and sit patiently by the light of the antique lamp as he read from the Bible, translating words she didn't understand to French for her. They loved to hear one another speak. He would explain the creation of the Earth in detail to her from his scripture. How in the beginning, the earth was formless and empty, darkness was over the surface of the deep, and the Spirit of God was hovering over the waters. He went on to explain that God created masses of dry ground he called land, and eventually Adam and Eve.

Great debate was a steady constant in their relationship, and they both found exponential growth in one another's knowledge, for their stories always complimented one another.

Evelyn would eventually tell Adam of the Oxychana practice and the visions she had. She told him of her earliest encounter with the Earth Mother at age eight and both she and Adam reveled in the astonishing similarities of their Creators.

"It is funny that your beliefs begin above the waters. Ours begin with the water too, but water *is* the deity." She would explain.

She explained how these waters were imbued with consciousness of the Mother and that torrent upon torrent of indescribably fast movement within herself produced friction, heat, and eventually fire. That the fire could not mix with the surrounding waters and fought its way to the surface exploding forth and bringing with it steam which became the air and then cooling—fires on the surface—became the earth. She explained that this was only possible through the Earth Mother's will, and that man carried with him this same will, or spirit which her people called 'the fire to live'.

He was astounded when she went on to explain that her people believe that each human being is but a perfect reproduction of the Earth Mother, and that their bodies are alive in the same way that she is.

He would counter with a scripture from his Bible, "Then God said, 'Let us make mankind in our image, in our likeness, so that they may rule over the fish in the sea and the birds in the sky, over the livestock and all the wild animals, and over all the creatures that move along the ground'."

They would laugh together and connect on an unseen level.

They had long conversations about other countries and their beliefs, and he found it particularly interesting that her tribe saw the separation of Pangea, into the landforms today, a result of man's modern ways of segregation, especially racially. It was then that he sparked a deep untold interest in her and began thinking passionately about her. He learned her on Alfred Wegener and his discovery of plate tectonics, and compared their theories on the movement of landmasses. They were one another's teacher, and before long she had begun speaking English quite well.

It was on the night that Adam had slipped climbing from the shower, his knee still too weak, that she fell for him entirely. She found him naked on the bathroom floor with but a towel pulled loosely over him to hide his more private parts. She had already gotten into one of the many lavish nightgowns which he had purchased for her—always they had picked out together.

She knelt beside him in the puddled water, unconcerned for her gown, shaking him softly. When he came to, he was looking up at her through slowly focusing eyes. Water had traveled up the light blue material of her gown and he found himself moving in a way that she could see him exposed. Her eyes sought the towel and the exposed flesh of his inner thigh and when they turned back to his face, her cheeks in a blush, his lips were waiting.

***

The cherry blossoms were in full bloom and the sun was shining warmly overhead on the day of their wedding. The white chairs and lattice gazebo on the green lawn, and the pink trees among them were a sight to behold. Mohammed gave her away, and they were united in holy matrimony under God, who she'd come to know well through Adam.

In the following days, Adam began walking without so much as a limp, and by the end of Sixty-nine, when the war was in a state of stalemate, they received word that Mohammed was granted increased British support.

The Nigerian federal forces were to launch their final offensive against the Biafrans on December twenty-third. It was to be a major thrust by the Third Marine Division, under the command of Colonel Obasanjo.

Obasanjo was to become President if the attack succeeded in splitting the Biafran enclave into two by the end of the year. Mohammed was very close with Obasanjo and found this to be an opportunity for more power. However he did not want Obasango to be a cruel leader, and so had already attempted to sway him toward the side of Christianity. To achieve this effort, Adam was asked to serve alongside Mohammed one last time. In debt to the man, he accepted, and Evelyn and Adam were, in turn, to be separated for the duration of his duty.

The nights were lonely for Evelyn and the days were long. She would pass her time reading Adam's books, and twisting the wedding ring on her finger as if wishing on it to bring him home. There had been no word from the South for almost a month and she was growing weary with worry. Being alone left her to think of her mother and father, who now seemed light years away, though she could cover the distance by truck in less than an hour if such trails existed.

She started a hobby of painting. Her first colorful image revealed the face of the Crone staring back at her, reminding her of the Fae's allure. The Crone always came bearing gifts, and perhaps her skillful hand was but another. The thought also brought back the memories of the years spent in the world of the Fae with the Maidens, the beautiful, and of course—her mother. Things *did* always occur in threes.

She had gone to the annex to pick up more canvas the day she heard that the war had ended. It was January 15, 1970.

Evelyn stood in front of her canvas and easel making small strokes with a fine brush, trying to bring out the highlights in his eyes. She wanted it perfect for him when he returned.

Mohammed watched her from the window by the entrance, leaning her face close to the canvas, completely enthralled. He didn't want to knock, but he knew it would eventually have to be done.

Evelyn sensed something and grew still. It had been but a few days since word of the war's end and she was expectantly awaiting her husband's return. Then she heard the knock on the door.

'Just like Adam!' she thought to herself.

Her heart skipped a beat and she smiled cheek-to-cheek as she dashed to the door. She held her dress up and her paintbrush with her left hand, the wooden palette in her right. Moving the brush to her right hand and gripping it with her thumb she flipped the latch and slung the door open with bright eyes.

Mohammed stood in the doorway with his hands outstretched to her, and the blood ran from her cheeks as she realized what he held.

The wooden palette slipped from her hand and clattered on the stone floor. There ... in his hands ... was Adam's Bible.

VII

First Encounter

It was well past noon when Jesse awoke. Evelyn lay only inches from him, her eyes still peacefully shut. She had pulled her knees up close to her chest during the night as if comforting herself.

Jesse slid out of bed, careful not to disturb her and cozied the comforter tight around her. He kissed her temple softly, and after throwing his robe around himself, made his way out of the room for the lobby. He looked back at her once more before closing the door quietly.

The thermos that was set out along the wall in the lobby every morning when he awakened was still there. The tea had most likely not been attended in a while, but it'd do. Surprisingly still warm, he stirred a bit of milk into two of the styrofoam cups. The lobby was peaceful today. He supposed everyone else was already about his or her daily grind. Only he and Evelyn had stayed up till daybreak. Nodding to the lad at the counter, who was now rounding the end toward the tea—probably to take it up for the day—he headed back up the steps.

The girls from room six were making their way to the lobby as Jesse topped the staircase. The leading one, dressed in denim jeans, a fur-collared pleated coat, and black gloves smiled at him as she approached. His back to the wall, he sidestepped to make room for those walking in proximity. He was holding the small styrofoam cups close to him as they passed. The trailing girls eyed the two cups of tea as they passed by, and smiled at him while exchanging glances and giggles.

When they had gone, Jesse looked down at the two cloudy cups of tea in his hands and smirked. Covering the final paces to his door, he tucked the cup from his right hand in-between his chest and forearm and carefully turned the knob and entered the room.

He put his cup on the table and slid one of the chairs to the bedside where he could see Evelyn clearly dozing. He put a hand on her shoulder and shook her lovingly. She stirred and, with a hand on his, turned on her back and looked at him.

He sat there with a warm cup of tea and a smile that was warmer yet, "It is late. They had almost taken the tea up when I went down, but I managed us a cup apiece." Jesse held the cup up before her, and she sat up, holding the blanket over her bosom like a beach towel. "Here, have a sip of this. Tell me if it's any good."

Evelyn laughed and took the cup in her hand, "So that is your plan, eh? Wake me with a spoiled cup of tea, and use me as your test dummy? I have never been treated more like a queen."

She smiled playfully and sipped.

Jesse leaned, reaching dramatically over to take his own cup from the table, "You cried out in your sleep. Were you having bad dreams?"

She pinched the comforter under her arms and lowered the tea in both hands to her lap, "I was back in the infirmary with Adam, when he introduced me to Mohammed." She paused, shook her head, and then looked up at him. "I'm sorry. You don't want to hear this now."

"No, I would love too. What else is there to do? I have safe tea. Please."

Beyond Jesse, she could see the icicles hanging from the shop's eaves across the street. The snow had melted just enough in the splendid afternoon sunlight, that the roof's patchwork was showing through clumps of sliding slush.

The window illuminated the room in a way that the dust seemed only present in the thick beams of light. It was in this way that the sunlight had poured through the doorway of her home, casting a shadow of Mohammed into the very entryway, on the day of the life-changing and horrible news.

"After Adam died, during the last offensive strike, Mohammed became a frequent visitor to our home. He was a very busy man with Obasanjo coming into presidency, but every chance he got he would take time to come and sit with me, admire my artwork, and talk over cocoa. It was only a couple of months until he would suggest that I take my husband's savings, which were considerable, and travel.

"There were people moving West after the war and Mohammed had struck some sort of a deal with an outside company to build a residential community not far North of the base. He said that he would never build South of where they were then, due to my family, and with the war now over, he assured me that they would always be safe."

Jesse had been sipping his tea, and hanging onto every word. But he felt uneasy about this story that Mohammed and Obasanjo could just forget about Evelyn and from whence she came. Why would they not try to benefit in some way, from the simple people of the Oxychana? He thought about it only a moment and then brushed it off, instead asking her, "You didn't want to go back with your money and help your mother and father, perhaps tell them where you had been all this time, and what you had seen?"

Evelyn put her cup out in a gesture that Jesse take it for a moment. Jesse obliged.

She stood up, tugging the rest of the striped comforter around her like the old kangas, which she was once so used to, and made her way through the small doorway to the loo. Leaning in close to the mirror over the sink she took in the sight of herself.

Smudging the stripes of mascara under her eyes away she said, "I had thought, if Adam and I were to have conceived a child, then I would take him to them and tell them what had befallen me. But when Adam died, I just couldn't bring myself to return. I had not found the one man who was born of the Sun. I had not conceived a child. Nothing was true. Nothing that I had been raised to believe was occurring. What was I to return as, a disappointment—evidence that our beliefs were wild and out-dated?"

She turned toward him and propped herself against the vanity staring at him.

"Evelyn. You had seen more than most of your tribe by then. Regardless of your running away, what could be said of your father who left on a constant basis? Now, you had stories of your own to tell."

Jesse thought of his own mother that he had never known.

"It doesn't matter, now," she said, moving elegantly back to him and her teacup.

Jesse stood and pushed the chair up to the table, "Take it from me, sweetie. If I had but just one chance to know my mother, it would mean the world to me. You don't think about going back, even now?"

Evelyn laughed softly, "After all these years? Even if Obasanjo had kept his promise and left my tribe to their own vices, they could have long since moved on themselves. Besides, this from someone who left his father in America because he couldn't bear the sight of his deterioration, most likely when his father needed someone most?"

She grew stiff and silent at those words, acutely aware that she shouldn't have spoken them.

Jesse turned from her and took a long draught from his tea, emptying it and tossing it into the small basket beside the kitchenette.

He felt her hand come over his shoulder and around his cheek, turning him into her. Her eyes, like polished emerald olives, expressed sorrow to him. Her hand on his warm cheek, she spoke.

"I'm sorry. I shouldn't have said that."

"It's okay. If I'm anything like him, I'll be forgetting it in a few days, anyhow." He managed a forced smile and kissed her lightly.

"What do you say, get cleaned up and see a show tonight? I know of a very hidden gem out in Windsor called the Theatre Royal. It is but a barn of sorts, but the playbills are quite astonishing."

Just then a rap on the door caught their attention and they both looked in the direction of the sound. Jesse went and pulled open the oaken wooden postern.

Gerald's wife, the chambermaid, entered, "I'm just here to clean up a bit, Mister Bankole. Is now okay?"

She eyed Evelyn wrapped in the bedding and then glanced at him.

"Now is fine," Evelyn stated. "If—with Mister Bankole's permission—I could take his quilt for company across the way." She stressed his last name in a way that marked her approval of it, and slid between the two into the hallway, making sure to keep herself covered tightly with the thick pinstriped material.

"Yes, uh, just return that at your earliest convenience, Ma'am," belayed Jesse innocently after her, poking his head out from the door and smiling—this time genuine.

"Of course," she said and mouthed to him, 'see you soon,' followed by a wink.

The maid went about changing his ice bucket and emptying his trash. Jesse, all the while, began rummaging through his closet for some warm clothes (no top hat this time) before heading for the shower.

***

It was five o'clock when Jesse made his way to the lobby.

Evelyn sat in her usual spot, puffing on a cigarette. She wore a thick red coat of suede and thigh-high boots over black leggings. The hat she wore might easily have fashioned a veil, but there was none. It was a shallow wide dish of black, which resembled a low sombrero.

She truly was a sight to behold. She was talking with one of the gentleman that had been inebriated the night before and pleasantly nodded at his conversation. He seemed sober now, which was a relief.

Evelyn laughed at the gentleman and leaned back into the sofa, only then noticing Jesse in his blue jean jacket, a bit of tan showing from under it. He was moving toward them, and her smile faded along with her interest of her current friend. The jacket was cut a bit short, and the jeans fit tight to his physique. His slick black shoes and belt even further complimented his penetrating eyes.

"If you'll excuse me." Jesse heard her say to the man while she rose, and watched him nod reverently after her.

As Evelyn moved to Jesse, he briefly met the eyes of the man—no hatred there. He felt tension, that he had been unaware of, melt away as Evelyn took his arm in her elbow. Jesse paused a moment as she extinguished her cigarette in the small aluminum tray, providing her the time needed to grant a return farewell nod to her newfound friend.

The snow still covered much of the grass, but the roads had been cleared well enough. The wind was chilly as the hour grew late. A black Austin awaited them curbside with the ever-present orange glow on the roof. Jesse turned the handle down and pulled the door open for Evelyn before he guided her into the back of the taxi. In a few moments they were off to Windsor.

***

The theatre was abundant with residents. The playbill showed 'PEOPLE' the musical, to be performed. It was a small cast of only six, but the reviews were excellent. And, as Jesse had told Evelyn, it was a gem. The building, which housed the stage, did have quite a barn-like feel to it, but the people who attended were dressed in the finest attire. High heels and shined boots tracked globs of mud into the ticket pavilion just inside the double doors. But beyond the turnstile, Evelyn drew in a quick gasp of air at the vaulted ceilings and sheer size of the seating. It must have taken thousands of bolts of red suede to make up the plush curtained ceiling and walls. A small bead of lights ran the length of the two aisles within, then straight down to the stage, reminiscent of an airport runway guiding its pilot in.

"Come down here," Jesse said, tugging Evelyn down toward the front. "I think there are some seats free there, up close."

The theatre glowed with only a soft orange light, making the red cotton seats stand out. They were inlaid in solid bench-style, oaken rows, cascading up behind them like a giant had opened its mouth and rolled its tongue out to the stage, the doorway atop the walk being a hollow into its throat.

"Here," Jesse said, helping Evelyn down in the front, just a few seats from the outside row.

The stage stood majestically in front of them. A well-polished oak of the lightest color, rounded and planed to form intricate molding along its edge. The now-closed curtain hung heavily in anticipation, echoing the exciting anticipation of the crowd for the opening act. Evelyn and Jesse would be able to see all but the very deepest recess of the stage floor. The layout was astounding! Evelyn loved the way the inside counterpart of this theatre reflected nothing of the outer. It made her think again of her first encounters with Adam.

Now the seats were filling with people, some in their green evening gowns sparkling like emeralds, others in pressed pants and top hats. But *her* Jesse stood out among them all in his blue.

There was *another* man who wore other than black attire. An odd gentleman two rows back. And who was that he was with? The girls. The girls from room six. Dressed in their fur and fluff, all three were tucked in around the man in blue and purple satin, fixed with a mint tie around his neck.

Nudging Jesse, Evelyn gestured in their direction smartly, "It's the gigglers."

Jesse was more preoccupied with the monocle the man in the plum suit was fingering as he poked playfully at the girls.

"Don't stare, Jesse. They'll recognize you."

"I'm sure they've already seen us," Jesse said as he waved to them playfully.

The girls nudged each other now and pointed in their direction, clearly going on with the man about how they had seen them in the hall together and *this very morning*, having tea together. This left no question to either of them that their musical lovemaking late last night had not only been *their* secret.

"Well," Jesse said to Evelyn, "it appears those three aren't the only noisemakers in the village, and a man with them; not exactly their style, eh?"

She grabbed at his sleeve and smiled. With a devious laugh, she pulled him close, "You had better watch it, Mister Bankole. I could easily put it off as your making all that ruckus alone."

"No one would dare believe. Besides, I have witnesses now."

Their cheeks touching one another, he threw one more noticeable eye to the trio before turning back to the opening curtain as the lights dimmed.

VIII

Budding Relationships

The play had been about love in and out of marriage. It tore away the façade of the comfortable middle-class marriage and Jesse and Evelyn had laughed at the characters' efforts to sort out their tangled emotional relationships while trying not to break up the family altogether. But now the cast was busy backstage preparing for their signings and after-party.

The lights had come full on in the theatre and the people shuffled themselves into single file lines leading up and out of the auditorium, as chance became them. In the front row they sat patiently waiting for the silk and satin oceans of various color to river their way through the doors and into the summit which was the lobby.

In the entryway waited the strange man in the purple get-up with his three female counterparts, all feverishly engulfed in conversation with one another. They had positioned themselves in a way that there would be no avoiding them should Jesse and Evelyn try and exit.

The inevitable conversation took place just as the girls had planned. They had sparked a subtle interest in Evelyn that Jesse would not yet know. The odd man, who they came to know as Greg, was a friend they had only just met, and he already had the three girls agreeing to follow him into Greece by train, in order to watch a spectacular circus, which was to be held there next month.

What delightful freedom they each could easily share together, Evelyn thought. It was commonly this way with upper-class, though. When you have a great deal of money to spend, you find yourself in the company of others whom also enjoy financial flattery.

Jesse remained quiet through much of the conversation, offering only a simple nod or smile, perhaps a laugh when it was appropriate. His attention remained on Evelyn, and the way she listened so intently to the girls' accusations and sly remarks. It was all in good fun, and after a while their ice-breaking comment, "Well, haven't you two grown quite fond of one another?" seemed innocent, and the fact that they had taken an interest in them harmless enough.

The interaction in the lobby led them all to a restaurant in central London where they spoke late into the night. Greg's limousine had been a lovely touch to the evening, fitting them all comfortably within and providing them tonic early on their way to the diner.

A light dinner and drinks had Jesse smoking Evelyn's cigarettes alongside her. This was not a thing Jesse would ever have been known to do, but the company's presence clearly had him in a state of malleability. He wouldn't know it now, but cigarettes would eventually become another vice of his.

The playfully casual experience with their four young newfound friends left an impression on Evelyn that grew within her like a sprouting seedling. First pushing her closer to Jesse and strengthening her fondness of him, then blossoming thoughts of warm love.

As Jesse watched, he could see the wheels turning in Evelyn's mind. She would sidelong glance at the girls while he was involved in conversation with Greg, as if trying to hide her timid smiles to them. But he felt her growing closer to him as she clutched tight his arm from her chair a mere fraction away. He wondered was her growing warmth a product of his attraction, or due to her own fear of fully opening herself up to the overly-friendly trio.

Evelyn indeed wondered what she may be capable of were she devoid of inhibitions entirely.

Halfway through the night it became overly apparent to them that the girls had no sexual attraction to their escort, but it didn't seem to bother the man in the slightest. Perhaps he was simply enjoying the company of them all as well. They were quite enthralling, with their bright smiles and ever-familiar giggles. Not so annoying as they were through the poorly-insulated walls of the hotel.

Greg's pale skin shone in the dim light of the diner. As far as facial hair, he had none, not the slightest hint of a pore, even when magnified beneath his classy monocle. But one would likely overlook this simple detail in contrast to his golden eyes, like amber, sealing tight air bubbles in its age.

Jesse had not witnessed him eat a bit, merely push his food about on the copper plate. Though he could not tell for sure, the breast of foul now was scattered, and looked as if it had been picked at by a vulture.

Greg had, however, heartily shared in an expensive bottle of wine, which now was nearing empty. It may have been a touch of the drink that brought Jesse to decide, but when his head was clearer he would find that it was the way Evelyn looked at those women and how he himself was intrigued by this extravagant fellow.

“So you all are to attend a show in Greece next month?” Jesse asks, now grinning full on and leaning into the table, his glass of wine in hand.

“The ladies have concurred, yes.” Greg makes a sweeping motion with his glass as he leans back against the velvet cushion of his chair, “It is to be the extravagant traveling circus!” He boasts as if he were the ringmaster himself. “They have been through two years ago. I can only imagine the things they have come up with since. It should be quite the spectacle!”

Glancing at Evelyn, still clutched tightly to him, Jesse motions for a toast.

“Well, then I must propose we meet again next month for the circus in Greece. If God wills it, you should fall victim to our company again, in a different land.”

The group came to life in agreeance. With their glasses raised to the middle of the two small round tables, which had been positioned together for the party, Evelyn interceded.

“A different land, yet part of the same great Earth.”

She tilts her head, smiles and then gestures they continue.

All the glasses come together in a harmonious melody, reminding her once more of those Christmas bells from her father’s stories, and in unison they cheer, “To Greece!”

***

The buildings passed by the window of the limosine as the occupant gazed out. His chin propped in the cup of his hand while he thought.

Greg had spent nearly an hour outside of the Brunswick Inn, his limosine parked, the party within talking into the first hour of the morning before evryone's departure. Such energy the couple resonated. Even more so perhaps, than Adam.

Generally, Greg did not intermingle with affairs of the Fae, but he had been engaged with the trio since his visitation with the Crone. His debt was nearly paid, but it offered him no comfort after seeing the Mother's plan now in its prime.

Watching the slowly advancing scenery, bathed in twilight and peppered with an occasional pedestrian on foot, he felt as if he had moved a hand on Father Time's clock and now was eternally doomed to calculate the missing seconds each minute time moved. It was becoming apparent that once you had manipulated fate, it turned into a full-time hobby, or would turn out a massive sacrifice.

He would finish his duty tomorrow evening and then decide if he should make due or cut his loses.

***

The brightness of Greg's spotless tuxedo contrasted drastically with the twirling yellow dust in the small shop's musty interior. Just past closing time he had silently arrived within the confines of the shop, displacing plumes of motes into an updraft past the yellow streams of thick setting sunlight which intruded through stained glass. The bundled old woman took no alarm in the odd appearance of the man, for the sight of such magical surprises were not foreign to her.

"You are here for something more, Djinn?"

The face of the Crone would surely frighten a Christian missionary, as it did he back before his transaction had been completed with her. Her face, though human, was lined in a way that could have never been natural for her age. Her hair was silver and rolled into a ball upon her head and she moved slowly but with dignity, unafraid.

He spoke to her with words, though he knew already what she would respond.

"No." he answered deftly.

"You have it then?"

From his lapel he produced a small bundle of cloth and placed it into her outstretched palm. The lids of her eyes stretched wide with wonder.

"Yes, this is it ... I feel it." Her voice, through raspy breath, conveyed excitement.

"So, it is done then?" Greg continued, "I follow the thoughts of men out great lengths and the further I ponder them, the more loss I see myself suffering. You cloaked this *gift* in pretty assumptions and beckoned me to it through deception."

The Crone looked up from the bundle under thinning bangs of black, eyes like glassy cataracts, but still her sight clearly beheld Greg's human form.

“Oh, Christian. It was you whose heart was untrue to your cause. I warned you to be wary of wishes and gifts, but you pushed on.”

It was true. All the gold in South Africa had not been enough for him. And then to go so far as to take a life …

“I *want* nothing more from you. I have delivered it to you. After all of these years, I have no place left to put my faith. I can only wish to know passion again before the end.”

“Bah! You know with what you bargained.” The Crone's words held no weight over Greg anymore. Both the Crone and he knew the path that lay ahead for them.

"The bargaining should not have been ours to undertake. Adam was innocent, as was Evelyn."

The glamour of the shopkeeper was little interested in this same old conversation but nevertheless assured him once again, "Give and take. Reap and sow, Djinn. We are all among the remembered and forgotten. You knew this before our deal was struck. Eternity makes you weary, as does it I."

She rolled one milky eye up to meet his gaze, "Man's day has passed." The crooked woman guided herself around the glass display case with a wiry hand, "Father Time can only claim one subsequent round. The Mother's time has come at last."

When she looked back to where the Djinn had stood, only a whirlwind of colored dust was listening.

"Yes. Go to them Djinn. Protect her, but even we cannot know to where we will return."

Moving On

It had been three weeks since the show. Jesse had extended his stay at the Brunswick and their new friends had left immediately for Greece, which meant no more giggling to keep them awake at nights. Jesse, however, enjoyed the evening silence now, and took advantage of his time alone here with Evelyn. Late night card games in his room, and horse-drawn carriage rides during moderate nights were their favorite pastimes. He was happy. They *both* were happy.

Evelyn was learning his habits well. She picked up on subtle clues to his challenged memory. A repeated question here … the same ole story there … but the most prominent trait was his difficulty with names. Always he had to be reminded the names of their new aquaintences. So similar were their names, and so simple: Emily, Jessica, and Veronica. But he never struggled to describe a thing that he had seen with his eyes. Sometimes she would hear him chanting to himself in repetition. But, upon his promise, he would never forget her.

"Not in three lifetimes," he would say. "Nor my father."

Only once had she become frustrated with him, when he failed to remind her to stop in the bank before the week's end. It was his birthday not three days hence, and she had spied the perfect gift. She so wanted to get this extra-special trinket for him without his knowledge. But, they had already settled back at their room for the night, and the banks were surely closed 'til Monday morning.

They still had their separate rooms where they kept their personal things, but always shared a bed.

That was the first night they had ever argued. It was also the first night since their meeting that Jesse had left her alone, as he went to the old familiar pub, and sat with a glass of the old familiar ale.

As they spent their time apart, other forces were going to work that neither of them could imagine.

***

The smoke in the tavern was a thing Jesse had gotten quite used to since he had been in Evelyn's company. He wondered exactly what she was doing right now. Perhaps he shouldn't have just disappeared after she scooped her jacket up in one arm and left his room for hers. 'Right back to familiar ground,' he thought to himself. But he wasn't going to beat himself up over it.

The truth was, when she saw he had left, *if* she saw he had left, she would probably enjoy herself a time alone as well. They probably needed this little time apart, for both of them had practically grown together at the hip. But one thing was stuck in his mind like a splinter, and it bore deeper by the minute. There was *something* about the man he had passed on his way out of the Brunswick. The man was obviously intoxicated and Jesse had recalled his face with ease.

Sipping slowly on the draught, he watched the weather come alive on television. Another deep snow was threatening, and clips of last week's shut-in showed tires mixing snow with the roads' dirty, salted surface. The muck brought to mind the night the two unruly men had embarrassed the hotel clerk weeks earlier. It sent a chill down his spine.

Tossing eight pound on to the bar and lifting his long coat from the high-back stool, he made for the exit. He was recounting events of the month and in his mind's eye, he saw Evelyn sitting in the lobby with her *new* friend as she awaited him to escort her to the play. But this time he envisioned the man drunk, and Evelyn drowning her sorrows in the ever-available bottle of Johnnie Walker, which he kept in his room.

He had only been absent an hour at most, never enough time for Evelyn to have lost her composure from the drink. But they had already been deep into wine this very night, before their buggy had left them curbside at the hotel, *before* the heated argument ensued.

Jesse's pace quickened, pulling tight the neck of his trench coat and fastening the thick brown top button. He wouldn't run, and break a sweat in his fine clothes, but his steps were hurried. In his mind, he kicked himself for getting too comfortable with this kind of attire. Were he in his usual loose-fitting, Clyde & Foster premium sweat suit, he could have been confidently at a sprint and been prepared to move more freely if a problem arose.

It was because of this thought that he would remove his penny loafers at the door of the Brunswick Inn this time. Not to be polite, for Gerald was busy mopping the entryway, much like before, when his son had done his best to keep up with the careless men's entrance weeks ago. No, but because the motion of the mop and the look in Gerald's eyes told more of the story than Jesse needed to confirm his fears.

The sound of Evelyn's nervous voice met Jesse's ears halfway up the flight of stairs. The bumbling drunkard came to his view, just outside her door, as he cleared the fourth step from the top. He could see that she obviously was not entertaining the man, much to Jesse's relief, but rather she was pushing him away with one hand attempting to keep him from entering her room.

The man, whom he'd long ago read to be ignorant of life's consequences, was smiling and coaxing her as if she were an unruly child. Evelyn was doing her best at closing the door, but the imbecile had pushed his way half between the knob and the jamb. He had hold of her upper arm making it impossible for her to get loose.

Jesse was there in an instant. As soon as he made out her frightened expression and saw that her satin gown was torn at the neck, his fury moved his hands into action. Grabbing the heavy brute by his shirt collar, which was already in disarray from his own filth, Jesse pivoted and slung the man hard to his rear, knuckling into the forearm which grasped at Evelyn, causing the drunken male's fingers to immediately loosen their grip.

The man's surprised face winced in pain, and his other hand automatically reacted and moved to the place on his forearm, which Jesse had crushed with sheer adrenaline. Evelyn stumbled backward and pulled her torn gown upright, holding it closed with one hand. The foolhardy drunkard's back hit the doorframe across the hall with a thud and he was now in a half-sitting position, struggling to keep himself on his feet. The action must have intensified the man's inebriated state, for he was obviously not in a position to defend himself further, but Jesse gripped a handful of the man's greasy hair in his left hand and cocked his right, meaning to pummel the dirt bag—who needed to learn his lesson.

"Jesse!" Evelyn screamed.

In the next moment he felt the resistance of her holding his arm back from destroying the menace.

"Nothing happened, Jesse! He only just now knocked on my door. Look at the state he's in!" She held his elbow tight, aware now of the couple down the hall, who had cracked their door to spy on what was happening.

Gerald, whom was making his way up the steps from the front desk, had been in earshot of Evelyn's pleas, and he now saw the situation at hand. Quietly assuring the curious couple that everything was okay, he approached them.

Jesse slowly loosed the man as he saw Gerald coming up and took Evelyn in his arms.

"Brett, you damn fool! I told you not to be meddling with this man's woman. You're drunk and they obviously don't want a part of you! I've a mind to throw you out of here, myself." Gerald said to the dirty guy who now was pushing himself upright and wiping his sleeve across his slobbering mouth and beaded sweaty forehead.

Gerald gave him a stern push toward the lobby and turned his apologies to Jesse and Evelyn, "I told him when he began blathering about her, just to let her be. He gave me an empty-eyed nod before quietly claiming that he was going to retire for the night, so I thought that was where he was headed. But, when you came in the door and I was mopping, the look in your eyes told me there was going to be trouble if he hadn't taken my advice. So when I heard a thump, I came running. Ole Brett has been staying here long as I've been owner, but he has gotten worse on the drink this year. If you'd like, I could see it as a proper excuse to be rid of him."

Jesse looked at Evelyn, and she gripped his coat lapel in her fingers, staring up at him. She was warm; he knew the argument was in the past. He also knew he'd been in this place for far too long. With some reluctance, he finalized their decision.

"It's fine, Gerald. I think I speak for both of us when I say that it's about time we catch a train."

Growing Hearts

The next morning, Jesse waited as Evelyn packed her things into parcels, eyeballing him as she folded while poking fun at him, "It's not easy for a woman to find clothing she adores. I can't just leave my things in the room like some people!"

But this time he had buttoned the few suits that she seemed partial to in a garment bag that he could carry over his shoulder, and he found himself for the first time in many years toting boxes to a taxi for a move.

The impending snowstorm had held out a day, but the brisk wind kept them aware of its likelihood, as they stopped in a small café for breakfast. Little did Jesse know Evelyn's intent, but she had purposely picked this place so as to not let her precious gift to Jesse escape her.

As they sipped their tea, Evelyn secretly smiled in excitement. When they left here, she would take him next door, by the hand, to the trinket shop and make him purchase this wonderful delight.

"Look here, Evelyn. It's a flyer for the circus! Strange for it to be in the London Times, so far away from Greece." Jesse said, pulling the faded red piece of paper away from the bulk of the news.

"Maybe it is to pass through here as well. Does it say where it is to be held?" she asked.

"No, nothing. You see it's just a picture and a title." He handed it to her and finished his Danish, wiping his lips with a napkin.

"Hmm."

She drank the rest of her tea, and folded the paper to tuck it into her bosom.

"Are we done, then? I have something to show you."

The tiny silver bell jingled as they entered the musty shop. Its shelves were alive with the wildest array of fine dolls and items of hand craftsmanship. Each individual work was a treasure of its own unique quality.

There were fine carved wooden ships and puppets crafted from wool and lace. Atop a shelf was a giant shark, perhaps made of plastic, but far too real, the blue and white colors of its skin blending perfectly, as if it swam alive in the ocean still. A music box quietly played its rolling copper cylinder as the tiny dancer twirled above, and the array of ticking clocks instilled magic in the very air, which swam with dust in the light from the amber-stained glass windows. The pale, porcelain face of an eerie blonde-headed doll mocked Jesse with eyes that seemed to follow him as he passed.

A polished glass enclosure occupied the recess of the strangely warm shop, encasing silver trinkets upon purple velvet, awaiting their turn for a much-needed shine. He only noticed the short gray-haired lady at the counter when Evelyn spoke.

"Do you still have the piece I asked you to keep for me? Please say you do. It was just perfectly the thing I adored."

The bun of silver hair was twisted and sat atop the woman's head, like a perched bird snuggled into itself in the cold.

"Of course I do, dear. Let me just get it from the back."

Jesse watched as the wrinkled old lady parted the plastic beads that hid the doorway into what must have been her office-of-sorts. And in her absence Evelyn explained to him.

"I found this early last week and it was what I was so upset about. I needed my own money to buy it this morning, but the banks were closed because I forgot to get the chauffeur to stop. It was *my* memory, not yours. But that is behind us now. Many nights I lay wondering if you were to forget me, how devastated I would be, and I think it only necessary that we have something that links us, to one another. A marker for your memory—and mine."

Jesse thought for a moment, looking down into her eyes and held her hands lightly in his own. He would never forget her, but he knew he had been refusing to accept the inevitability of such things. He forced the thought from his mind and kissed her, not wanting to offer empty promises at a moment like this.

As the little elderly woman appeared amongst the rattle of the swaying beads, he glimpsed the intricate makings of the amulet resting among tissue in her hands.

The golden sun, attached to a simple black rope meant to fit around the neck, had been etched by the finest hand craftsman. The surface of the gift was made in a way to resemble the continents of the Earth. Alongside it was a charm of sterling silver, linked to a bracelet of fine metal loops. The charm was molded in the shape of a moon quarter full, a crescent with a nose and a smile, the chubby cheek of it bringing its face-like feature to life.

When the tissue fully blossomed upon the transparent countertop, Evelyn took up the moon with her soft fingers and with bright eyes reached to the blazing golden sun with her other.

"They are a pair, Jesse. Like you and I," then lifting them up, "yours, the sun that's filled with shining light that blazes far and wide. Mine, the moon, which reflects the sunlight back, but has no light inside. Together we can shine anew, a living breathing light. In union once again in life, that Mother Earth provides."

She fitted the moon perfectly atop the precious sun, and with a click, they were together. The moon now covered the ancient engravings of the continents and gave the illusion of Pangea. It was a perfect piece of them, an absolute reflection of their nightly religious debates on belief. They fitted so perfectly with the grand scheme of things that Jesse felt his head spin momentarily at the impossibility of it all. Something deep within him was welling up as if an ancient memory were waking from a long-time dream.

"Déjà vu," he muttered.

He picked up the relic and thumbed it, "Where did you get this Ma'am, if I may ask?"

"Oh, I'm not quite sure," she said with trembling hands, as she gathered up the tissue. "Some of these old things were here when I bought this shop. It was the added little bonuses that persuaded me to purchase."

She took a raspy gasp of air and pointed a slim, shaking finger to them, "If it is so remarkable to you, then it is yours. I can *see* when something fits just right with someone. Knowing it had found its rightful home is payment enough for this old soul. Not often do I see the cheer in young folks' faces anymore. My family has all passed, and I haven't seen a surprised Christmas face for some time. You would be doing me a great pleasure by taking it."

Evelyn's attempt at swaying the old Crone's decision didn't make it past the second moment. She would not take a shilling for it, and that was that.

For a brief second, Evelyn felt the veil of the Fae upon her, as something about the woman's generosity made her uneasy.

Jesse snuck an addressed business card from the desk before leaving for the station, and told Evelyn, on their way to the door, that *this* Christmas would be one that the lady would remember.

Closure

The hotel in Greece was a sight to see. It possessed every modern commodity that they could hope for. All around them was sheer white paint and marble tile, which decorated the floors and countertops. Their suite was massive—overly exotic for any couple—but they loved it. They felt at home.

In the lobby was a giant tree decorated for the seasons, it had huge golden spheres of sparkling glass and tiny little lights. Atop the fir sat an angel made of porcelain and fine satin, and they commented on it as they checked in. There was a smoking room, in the shape of a shallow cleft right out in the hall by the stairwell that wound its way up to the next floor.

It wasn't a week until the show and the couple wondered if they could be lucky enough to bump into their friends in the midst of such a busy city.

Evelyn had taken up painting again to pass the time. She loved the trinket they had been gifted by the sweet old lady, and they both kept it on their person at every moment. She wore the silver loop bracelet, and Jesse donned the amulet of gold, usually tucked beneath his garments close to his heart. It was the center of her current portrait.

Jesse always thought deeply about his father this time of year. It was nearly six Christmases ago when he left the last gift he would ever leave ... an elegantly framed photo of them together in the lobby of the hospital.

Evelyn, of course, had similar thoughts of her father, and remembered the first time she had seen snow, moving north from Africa. She had heard of how urban cultures celebrated holiday seasons but never had seen the annual decorations of such places, which had only recently just begun. The same flyer that she still had hidden away among her luggage, they now saw in each morning's press and frequently plastered on the boards of certain restaurants:

The 'Globus Circus', was announced an *international delight.*

The couple had grown quite accustomed to their new living space. Evelyn enjoyed her peace and quiet while Jesse went down to the lobby alone for a drink in the evenings. They would always seem to meet again at the cleft beside their room where they would sit and enjoy a cigarette together before bedtime.

They had assured themselves by the fourth night that they would come upon their company during the first show, which was to be held this coming Friday. Knowing Greg's lavish lifestyle, they likely would find him in the front row and he would most definitely be the oddest dressed. But it was on the fifth night that the most familiar sound beckoned them to leave their comfy spot on the soft, light-colored, padded sofas of the cleft lounge and then venture up the flight of stairs beside it.

With astonishment, Veronica had spun Emily and Jessica around to meet Jesse and Evelyn topping the shallow spiral stairwell from the lounge.

"Girls, look! There they are!"

The giggling had been so prominently ingrained in their minds after living at the Brunswick within nightly earshot, that they had both immediately caught it and met each other's gaze with a matter-of-fact look at one another.

"No way!" Jesse had said before they both had comically fought their way up the elegantly curving stairwell.

"I can't believe it!" said Evelyn, beaming with recognition and hugging Emily in a warm embrace.

Meanwhile, Jesse had taken the hand of Jessica and kissed it smiling, speaking in Veronica's direction, "We heard your voices from the smoking lounge downstairs, we stay directly by it."

"Did you just get in?" Veronica asked, while Emily and Jessica were admiring the silver charm on Evelyn's wrist.

"About a week ago."

Evelyn pushes her gift in for Veronica to see among the chatter, "Isn't it lovely? And it has the most amazing story behind it. Jesse has its counterpart in his shirt. Where's Greg?"

Veronica took Evelyn's wrist in her hand and with wide eyes surveyed the rare piece as Emily filled them in on their arrivals.

"He has been keeping us busy! We've been all around the city, and did you know he is the owner of the venue where the circus is on? He is quite interesting!"

The evening was already coming close to an end when they had happened upon the girls, for the trio already wore their comfortable nighttime attire and Evelyn's eyes were heavy. So weary, she had not noticed the same wide eyes that surveyed her silver charm also growing wide and trading glances with their company at the sight of Jesse's amulet.

After ordinarily complimenting Jesse on his jewelry, Emily and Evelyn went hand-in-hand back down to the lounge alone and Jesse took the opportunity to question Veronica about Greg's whereabouts.

Surprisingly he had been staying below on Level One in a much smaller suite. Perhaps, to keep a low profile, Jesse guessed, for it seemed the man was very well-known where they found themselves at the moment.

Jessica and Veronica disappeared into their room and Jesse slowly made his way back down the steps where he could see Emily speaking with Evelyn in overly-hushed tones. When she saw him approaching an unnatural silence fell over the two women.

Emily took her feet as Evelyn acknowledged him, "Honey, are you about ready?"

Emily nodded a farewell to Evelyn, and offered a weak bow as she passed Jesse for her room. His eyes followed her to the stairs before his cautious response.

"I think I will sit for one more cigarette. Go ahead, I'll be just a minute."

Evelyn pulled herself from the sofa and gently kissed him, "I'll be waiting."

Her eyes were still just as mesmerizing as the first night they had met and her lips—eternally drawing.

Jesse sat down heavily and took a deep draw from his cigarette. He was unsettled. His joy at meeting the girls again was genuine, no doubt in that. However, he felt Evelyn's fondness for the trio, especially Emily, was a growing animal, which if left untethered may grow too wild for him to control. He tried to push the thought from his mind. All that mattered was her happiness, and *that* she surely had. Besides, when he saw Greg he would feel considerably better, he knew this, and he would make it a point to visit him tomorrow. He palmed the medallion, which was his ever-present link to her, then extinguished his cigarette before joining Evelyn for the night.

Jesse did not bring up his unsettling thoughts to Evelyn that night but they got involved in a deep conversation about their families and once again the debate on visiting their fathers ensued. Jesse really didn't even know if his father was still alive at all. But Evelyn's argument on returning to the States one last time was considerably enticing and the suggestion only further worried him about her involvement with the three adoring lady companions.

Multiple times that evening, he eyed the phone on the bedside table, it urging him to call information—if he could even recall the hospital's name—and know the truth. He was sure that he had amply convinced Evelyn to take a party to Africa and seek out her mother and father after the holidays, if for nothing more but to introduce him. He would know everything about her if she would only surrender fully to him. In some ways, this she had done. It was Jesse's own uneasy doubts that were invisibly threatening the stable bond that was between them.

***

It was Friday afternoon and Greg had reserved a special spot for the party ringside away from the bustling bulk of the crowd.

The circus had been erected within the confines of an old coliseum where chariot races used to be watched in awe by the Greeks. It was set up in a way that the old stone-step seating could be utilized by the spectators who were not still busy shopping in the outer ring for cotton candy, peanuts, or popcorn. The variety of such things were available from vendors behind folding wooden tables, who were dressed in striped clothing and exotic headwear. Children ran about with spinning noisemakers and balloons. Dragon snappers popped on the littered floor of the grounds as parents strived to entertain their kids.

All the while, Jesse sat engulfed in conversation with his host, Greg.

In contrast to his former attire, Greg now seemed eloquently professional in stature. The monocle under his brow was the most prominent reminder that he was, indeed, the same man Jesse had been seated across from weeks earlier. Evelyn, as usual, held tight to Jesse's arm and eavesdropped on their exchange.

"How did you come to own such an extravagant venue, Mr. Dawson?" Jesse asked formally.

"I think we're past formalities. Please, call me Greg with all of the same abandon that our night of drinking allowed us."

Greg unbuttoned the collar notch of his cream-colored shirt.

Smirking, Jesse tilted his head in an accepting gesture, "Quite honorable, Greg. It's the penguin suit that threw me off. I half expected you to be in more, how can I say, eccentric attire. Excuse me for being presumptuous."

"No harm done. I met earlier with the conductor of the Globus to show my appreciation at his holding the circus here. As you can see, it is a huge endeavor and the revenue it produces pays for upkeep. As for how I came about owning this coliseum, my father passed it to me. He was a good man ... loved the old chariot races, and continued them late into his years. The seating, of course, grew quite sparse, but the tourists filled the stands in warmer months. We still do an annual running, today."

Jesse looked to Evelyn at his side and her eyes met his with understanding.

All the talk of family had Jesse wanting to flee for the States at once. His absent-minded years were now pressing on his soul, and he feared the worst. He feared that perhaps he would not be in time to see his father, that he would have passed at a time when Jesse had not so much as offered him a thought. But *surely* he would have received word. No, he knew there was no one fast enough to track him and his carefree changing lifestyle.

Never had he thought of inheritance until now. Other than the horrible memory gifted him from his father, other things passed down he had not considered.

Jesse shifted uneasily in his chair staring distantly in thought as Veronica and her friends broke into babble about the show starting.

Evelyn had been keeping Greg's attention but was aware that Jesse wasn't present among them, save his body. When the drums rolled, and the spotlight danced across the canvas of the massive tent, she shook him, "Jesse."

He turned to her, coming back as if from sleep, "I'm here. Sorry."

She smiled warmly at him and pressed firmly into the cavity of his chest.

A chord, and the ringmaster started, "Ladies and Gentlemen ...."

Though the couple sat amongst friends and entertainment, they both knew that they needed closure with their family affairs.

But, what Evelyn didn't realize was, in Jesse's mind, he was already homeward bound.

XII

The Map

Jesse had always been too giving. It was an honorable quality, but it was an attribute that kept folly on the constant edge of a knife. People are blind. Not entirely, but more dominant is their blindness, than their ability to see within the soul. But were they really to blame? No.

Jesse's nobility was ingrained so deep that it struck the utter quick of his being. So he would not blame them, or call them blind. Instead he would accept his own shortcomings and acknowledge that perhaps he was but an amateur at expressing his true intentions, and that speaking boldly about his wants was a practice that he found himself very weak at. This too though, was the nobility in him shining through, because he marked that particular flaw *not* as a flaw, but rather a denial of his own selfishness.

If there was a man who shared a loving God's attributes, it would be Jesse, but he would not dare admit this to himself or anyone else for that matter. He would not choose to be the one shining, but rather would share a dimly lit existence of his own doing by speaking humbly of himself and highly of others. This value, which he had picked up in Tokyo, was not always understood or appreciated. However, it was said (and this he believed) that it was exercise for the soul, a sure way to keep your soul in shape, while acknowledging your bodily desires. This practice had often replaced his more pronounced belief that 'To discipline the body was to feed the spirit' until finally overshadowing it and nudging it to a place years earlier in his past. It had helped him accept that the boozing was justified—spiritually. 'Even beliefs evolve,' he thought to himself, while lazing on the tan suede of the cleft sofa—alone.

The circus had been, as expected, exciting. The acrobats and the animals were particular favorites of his. A show would be a show though, and Greg had kept him excellent company. He found himself laughing, at first, with a bit of reserve but as the night pressed on and they once again circled a dining table for drinks, his laughter grew into nothing short of reckless abandon.

He had freed his arm from Evelyn's constantly faithful grasp in an attempt to express his trust in her; also to gain a bit of freedom for himself. But it was this act, coupled with his own distasteful judgement of himself, that would have him regret ever loosing her. It was ever since the gift she found for them, that these doubts gained life and began growing. The doubts were hidden in the shadows of his mind, blooming from the gift that now bound them to each other, the gift that even now he bore around his neck.

It was true that they had many a discussion on religion and creation, but it was Adam that the pendant truly reminded him of. For wasn't *he* the one who tutored her in English and the Bible, not Jesse? Of course, now he had passed on, but the spirit of the memory of Adam, for Jesse, seemed eternally linked to this mysterious jewel after hearing the vivid story of Evelyn's elopement and marriage to him. He had been sure that her age-old memory's burden flowed out of her with her words that night, but in some small way it had found its way into him.

Now, here he sat on the sofa that occupied a volume of the cleft room at the bottom of the steps, taking drag after drag from one of the cigarettes, which he had so easily phased into his addictions. He was here, among the smell of leaf tobacco and the sound of giddy upstairs giggling. Slowly recounting the events of the day following their circus debut, so as to burn the picture of this town's layout deep into his memory, he sat.

He saw, in his mind's eye once again, himself walking the sidewalk adjacent to the Grecian boulevard, his own reflection his companion when he passed the crowded shops. When there was no reflection, it was only his shadow which accompanied him. He had made his way, as Evelyn slept in late, down Poseidon Way and rounded the corner to the old marble hutch that marked the entrance to where he would find the local cartographer.

Initially, he had planned on giving the map to her on Christmas, which was but days away, but now he had come up with something else to gift her early, to gift her *now.*

Nursing the last night's hangover had brought him right back to swift decisions and that same reckless abandon, which he had kept dormant for so long. So when the prominent giggling breached his bubble of smoke from upstairs, once again, the *idea* (whether good or bad) shone crystal clear in his head, dominating his more fragile character and reminding him of his own belief in personal power. He intended to push the limits of the now wavering fine line between chance and fate.

Jesse had surely seen an abundance of strange and unexplainable happenings, which had brought about the déjà vu he had experienced in the old woman's shop not long ago. Things that, despite his memory problems, he *knew* were real and *had* happened. His developing disbelief in mere chance, a result of lengthy pondering on how nearly impossible the existence of the trinket was which lay against his breast, among a handful of other events just as miraculous, had proved there was more going on than he was only presently aware. A higher power planning this life perhaps, or making it come forth in some intelligent design.

Whether it be himself unconsciously creating and presenting these things in intelligent fashion or, as Evelyn saw in her beliefs, *another* being entirely watching from a distance but still remaining part of us, did not matter to him. What *did* matter was that he disturb the stagnant veil of simple peace, as to keep it from solidifying into a single form—to keep change in his life. What mattered more than anything now, was to never bore, to never assume to know what the future surely held, lest he diminish the gaping distance that his current beliefs presently possessed to work their infinite array of miracles.

The one prominent thing that this entire experience of existence had taught to him was that he could not be like Greg and predict with certainty what was going to happen, and know that it would. Because he found that once he limited himself to one *definite* course of action in attaining a result, he limited the possibilities of even more miraculous outcomes to present themselves along the way to the result itself.

It was in this thinking that Jesse began to drink more often than he should. He would find time to make his way down to the lobby and sneak a few extra tonics in before each night came to a close. Evelyn, of course, said nothing of his actions, she was comfortable in her room painting—at times meeting with Veronica for dinner or an innocent cigarette. Inside of Jesse though, a wildfire danced its unpredictable flame throughout the evenings, keeping him fashioning even further this *gift* he wanted her so to enjoy.

What he was to give her, he could not say if it was for Evelyn alone, or for himself. In a way, he wanted to test the impossible coincidences that they commonly found themselves in.

Love was a thing that he could pick apart for hours, from different angles, as he drank. One time, he looked at it from a direction of fate, and then another from a perspective of chance.

In his time, he had loved and lost like any other. First, of course, there was that childlike love that burned so bright with desire and lust, more than with devotion and sanctity. Those times, also like any other first experience, would not last, for the high temperatures in which that desire burned, consumed the love too quickly.

Then, he would be with a woman who loved him with a depth that he could not understand. Try as he might to please her, he soon found himself lost, changed, unsatisfied with his own self-growth as he stumbled time and time again, trying to hide his secret ambitions. The lies would eventually engulf that love in darkness.

Then, there was his last, the *one* he had found attractive and free. Now that he'd possessed a newfound knowledge of love, which his previous encounters so bestowed upon him, he'd known he was ready. He had been prepared to commit because he had come to think that commitment was the secret in a loving relationship. But that time it was *he* who would bear the scar of a broken heart, and wrestle through the tangled web of lies that his partner had woven to keep him safe from sorrow. Of course, that safety net would eventually break.

But this time it was different. It was something not only comfortable, but strange in how the two seemed so totally aligned to each other, something even *he* might come to believe was the work of a higher power.

The drinking would have to stop, and it would only happen if he could know for sure if *this* was his destiny. Consequently, in an effort akin to stiring up a hornet's nest—whether done in loss or love—he had decided. He had decided that, for a time, there would be no them, but rather he would steal some time again for he alone.

XIII

Letting Go

The music was playing in the upstairs apartment again, and the noise from the group of girls was noticeable, as always. They were obviously the happiest occupants of the Greek Chateau now, as well. The three girls loved each other like no other people could. They made love each night, apparent from the giggles and chants, and laughed through the midnight hours. It was a normal thing that everyone had gotten used to.

Evelyn lay beside Jesse in the bed, and they stared lovingly into each other's eyes. No one else could love like those happy girls, except maybe the two of them, who loved each other so deeply and had for a time now. But *he* knew she was curious to know what it felt like to be with those girls for just one night.

It was Greg who had eventually brought him to see this and he finally brought it up to her that evening. Of course, she would argue with him that he was all she ever needed, but he was determined to give her this *gift*—this freedom. Though in the back of his mind, it was an answer *he* was looking for, and the question was one that could not simply be asked aloud.

"I *do* believe I am entitled to an opinion," he had said during the conversation. "I am also entitled to a woman who is important enough to me that I allow her that freedom."

It had been true in his heart of hearts, and the truth in his statement shone through in an undeniability of the experience he was suggesting.

She had already stolen brief glances at the group of girls, trading happy gestures, and hitting that perfect cue of harmony with them, just never succumbing to their innocently disguised pull to enter their room—knowing where it would lead—in fear of sacrificing what she had with him. He trusted her more than any woman he had ever known, and had he not offered her this freedom, she would have never asked. That fact was but one of many among the reasons he had made the decision.

On the night, Jesse had raced to the top of the winding steps of the next story and found Evelyn looking into the room where the girls stayed, but it was empty. The scent of patchouli came from the open door.

They had already agreed, and the music had grown prominent over the last few nights and now hung constant. They should have definitely been up there now.

"This is foolish!" she said, suddenly running by and heading down the stairs back toward their room.

He tried reaching for her, when he saw Emily emerge from a room adjacent to theirs, "Wait, Evelyn! Here she is!"

Evelyn had stopped mid-flight when she spied the rest of the trio approaching from below, and, with some reluctance, walked slowly back up to meet him.

Emily had seen Jesse's demeanor and immediately realized his intentions. She politely excused herself from the inhabitant of the stranger's room and turned her attention their way.

Veronica and Jessica, young and beautiful, were dressed in their matching pajama pants and short-shorts, complimented by striped shirts, and were coming up the steps behind Evelyn, giggling as they ascended. The herbal smell which originated somewhere inside of their room seemed to stick to the linens they all wore.

Jesse backed into a recess in the hall and let the girls close in on Evelyn as he slowly let go her hand. The trio was crowding her and playing like teenagers at a sleepover.

Jesse thought he heard Emily ask her under-breath, "Are you sure you want to do this?"

Then couldn't help but imagine his Evelyn responding cunningly, "Are *you* sure you are *ready* for me?"

Before he could blink, they were holding hands in a line down the hall, and the last girl, Veronica, with dark hair like Evelyn's, leaned into the recess upon him.

"Now, I'm going to kiss you just this once ..."

Veronica kissed him perfectly on the lips, before entering the fragrant room and closing the door behind them.

The time had come for Jesse to make his preparations, which he did as Evelyn was distracted by her remarkable *gift*. When he had finished combing through all the details in his mind, he asked himself if he would finally be satisfied if the outcome of his experiment were to prove noble.

He could genuinely see himself settling down with this woman, and perhaps raising a family ... and yes, even giving up the drinking.

"Only time will tell," he said aloud, laying back onto the comforter, listening to the vague music, now only a lullaby above.

It was a long night, and he slept alone.

The morning came, and he could hear the laughter from the room. This time with Evelyn's unmistakable tune mixed in, though a bit hard to distinguish among all the rest. It wasn't but an hour that he had lain in the bed staring at the ceiling thinking back on all the relationships he had suffered, and all the *ends* of them. The one thing they all had in common was that they ended.

Evelyn eventually entered their room clutching a pillow to her chest. Her lips sparkled with a pink balm, and her mascara had run in an unusual pattern around her eyes. Leaning down, she kissed him.

Then standing erect again she inquired of him to his satisfaction, "Well?"

He looked at her, in her purple cotton pants and camisole then said what was only natural, "I can hear the laughter, the happiness. If you want, Evelyn—"

She clutched to the pillow tighter, "—It was only that once, Jesse; I told you. All I need is you. Wasn't it you that said you were entitled to your opinion and entitled to someone who deserves freedom? But if you want me to keep doing it, that is up to you."

She began very slowly moving toward the door.

"Wait!" he said. "It is the nature of things, you know. People love and then grow apart. It is the same everywhere, breathing in and out, ebb and flow, live and die. I think ..."

After a moment he continued, "You are just as important as I am and you, more than anything, are entitled to your own happiness. We all are entitled to seek our own happiness. And happiness is the most important thing in life."

He watched as she bit her bottom lip and turned away, back to the room upstairs, perhaps to say her final thanks, perhaps to enjoy another tumble.

Jesse rolled onto his back exhaling heavily and pulling loose the comforter, his eyes staring at the space above him on the ceiling with no genuine concern either way.

In the distance he heard the music from the room amplify as giggles silenced, and this time he could pick out the words inside the tune as it played:

Pieces of your broken heart,
It's what you've done from the start,
Come together, and
Fall apart,
Come together, and
Fall apart,
Come together, and
Fall apart.

Shaking off the eerie feeling of the magical occurrences, as of late, he pulled out the map, which had been intended for her, and still was. But there was something missing from it. This map, which once intended only to direct her to a place, would now also bear a *time.*

"If we are connected to one another Evelyn, by this device we so blindly stumbled upon, God shall see us fit to meet again."

Excitement pumped through his veins as he finished scribbling the note to her then tucked it into the leather-bound folder, which housed the map, a location, date and time. He knew she would take a time for herself among the girls, when she discovered he had departed, but it was necessary. He needed this time for closure.

He had pre-planned to fly back to the States and see his father a final time, and it was only best that she didn't lay eyes upon him. Perhaps secretly his actions came from a place of disgrace. He was in fact afraid that if she saw the future him, she would come to consider herself not strong enough to handle it?

Was he afraid she would flee, after conjuring her own excuse in place of that fear? It didn't matter. What was done was done! If it was willed, it would be. When he closed the book on his past, he would return to her and see her in her birthplace, if it was written.

Perhaps then they would both know for sure, if fate had set them on the same path. But then there was always the chance that this all was simply a thing of his imagining, another foolish fairytale? Who knew? Maybe her mother *was* full of *real* magic, and *could* see the future; Jesse was starting to think that crazier things had happened. But would his father still be there after all these years?

XIV

The Journals

The flight into New York was just another lengthy stretch of time in which Jesse pondered over all that had befallen him in the recent months. Evelyn, of course, was the only real thing of substantial subject matter that he coherently willed into the depths of his precious mind for safe-keeping. He had promised and wouldn't allow himself to forget her. Though she knew of his teetering memory, he had never really conveyed to her the true nature of the disease which made it difficult to capture important events more permanently.

As Evelyn had spent time with Jesse, as would be with any normal healthy person, more memories of togetherness built within her, but with his mind it was a different. His short-term memory was horribly scarred now, and if he hadn't spent adequate time focusing on the most precious moments, they would have been gone in days.

He had laid awake beside her many nights wrestling his attention from her slowly rising and falling chest and peaceful face, which he so dearly loved to watch, because he knew he must dedicate his undivided attention to the repetitive process of his 'memory-burning'—he had come to call it—lest the precious time they shared be in vain.

Jesse would be bothered by the loneliness if he allowed himself the pleasure of self-pity, but he wouldn't. He found comfort despite the constant chatter of the first-class passengers, in recounting the eloquence in which his vague goal had been unfolding. Though he knew that he could never choose the exact path he would take to get there, he still held fast a constant goal in mind, and always his positive outlook on it was productive. He found hope in the knowledge that past kings, in their eras, had never known *how* they would become a great leader, they just knew that they one day would. By those means, had the magic thus far happened; only a fool would try and fix a clock that wasn't broken. So on he would go about his adventure the same way he had always gone … with faith.

The man across from Jesse looked up from his newspaper when a broad smile spread across his peaceful face. He must've had a fleeting thought of judging him a well-dressed madman before his eyes shifted away. Jesse was smiling, in a cunning type of fashion because finally he felt *he knew* what he was doing.

This was the first time in all of his travels that he felt as though he may have found some true adventure at last. Up until meeting

Evelyn, had been only leisurely time-consuming vacations like a tourist, turning a blind eye to the fact. But this trip had a purpose, and the next would be a vaguely uncertain journey back to her.

It scared him just enough to excite and enliven him, as if he had regained his youth. How he'd played the last card is what brought the maniacal smirk that had caught that man's attention.

He had left Evelyn so suddenly, while knowing she adored him deeply and eternally. It had to happen for the adventure to find him, but he wasn't leaving her entirely alone, no. She would be safe in the company of wealthy and attractive people where she belonged.

She would be comfortable, in a physical sense; it would be the mental absence of him that may (or may not) drive her to wish adventure on herself, as well. Yes, everything was as it should be. The last thing he would allow was himself fall victim to negative thoughts of her possible abandon. Clutching the golden sun beneath his shirt, Jesse recalled her words and thought, 'The sun is filled with shining light … and you reflect it back. So I am to lead. You are to follow.' His grin again was renewed with life as the seatbelt light came on with a ding.

***

Finding his father should be simple enough. He need only have to visit the post office box, where there's sure to be a bill from the hospital stating its address. An address lost among the weathered sponge that was his mind. The post office and box number was something he would carry with him until the end. Twenty-second Street, in box twenty-two, as in twenty-two years old, when he finally accepted that he would never know his mother. Yes, he would at least remember that.

"Damn!" The box had been crammed full of useless litter, a collection of his absent years.

"And more crated in the back awaits," the postman informed him.

He had no use for *that* mail.

Sliding a garbage can to the box, Jesse disposed of the bulk and shuffled through what may have been checks or bills, or both, with little more than a thought of such things. He was on a mission and when he came across the sure-fire sign that this was it—a blue symbol of a serpent coiled around a sword and crossed shield—in the return address portion of the envelope, he held it aloft in victory.

"Yes," Shaking the envelope with his left and nodding.

He had it.

It was time for him to know the truth.

The postman wasn't exactly eager to give him directions to the address, but he obliged after forcing Jesse to approve his disposal of the abandoned collection of rubbish, and only after a lengthy explanation that there was to be no forwarding address updated.

But, to his dismay, the hospital had discharged his father to a nursing home some years ago, after they had managed to finally find a regular dose of controlled medication that kept him stable. He was to be housed in a memory care unit, but at least it was something.

Jesse sat in the heated taxicab, staring at that building, whose double doors sat motionless, bathed in the light of an orange cone spilling from an overhead fixture. He was in there. His likely future was in there waiting to stare him directly in the face.

'And what if he doesn't rememb—no—don't allow yourself to What if. Just get out, and walk in there.'

Now it was Jesse's boots that dripped muddy slush upon the entrance of this warm reception area. Stomping his feet had totally been absent from his mind as he entered there, and the salted snowy parking lot of this New York retirement home had followed him haphazardly in the door.

Jesse privately laughed at himself, smugly finding irony in the way he'd judged the brute on the first night he met Evelyn. At least, however, *he* was composed. Not sober ... but composed.

As he approached the receptionist, he pulled the paperwork the hospital had given him from his slicker and passed it to her with a gloved hand. He glanced back over his shoulder and could see the beaming headlights of the cabby through the glass doors one hundred yards off, surely waiting for him as he'd asked. But why had he had him wait? Wasn't he here to visit, to gain some closure, as Evelyn had put it? It was time to stop fooling himself.

The lady uncertainly glanced at the name on the document. After meeting his eyes for a split second, she nervously went to her file cabinet.

She knew something. She knew something and didn't want to come outright and say it, and so she shuffled through her files looking for a bit of paper evidence for back-up.

Jesse waited patiently as she struggled to find the words. He had almost come to the brink of saving her the discomfort of informing him the ill will, when she had it.

She produced a manila folder stuffed thick with rubber-banded medical records, on the front, a black-and-white photo of what could have been Jesse in thirty years. But the photo was not of Jesse. It was of James Bankole, his late father.

There was no crying. Perhaps only a momentary hint of terror; a premonition of himself one day suffering the fate of the same oblivious dialing out-of-sorts.

He had learned from the file that his father had been cremated. There lay no site at which he could go and weep and pray and so there would not be such things, at all. Only the tiny orange envelope that came from the rubber-banded bundle kept the momentum of his journey moving in a forward, never-faltering, and goal-oriented direction. For that at least, he was thankful.

As the sleet stuck outside the cabby's icy spidered window, Jesse turned the silver key in his hand while reading aloud to the driver the address of the bank, which was printed on the envelope itself. A safe deposit box. And once again the ever-present feeling of perfection gave him goose bumps, while he read the number engraved into the silver … twenty-two.

***

The next morning was accompanied by a feeling of direct intent. There was no time for a headache. A quick swig of last night's brandy, and Jesse knew precisely where it was he was headed. Of course, the bank ... but not directly. First, he would make a quick stop and get out of the clothes which had been encumbering for far too long. He was a man on a real mission now, one with mysterious undertones, and he needed his old comfortable fashion as his companion. It just felt right to him, purchasing and donning his new $1690 Dolce & Gabbana sweat suit. He was Jesse again, but a *new* Jesse, with purpose.

Number twenty-two, the box the key fit into, was not at all what he had expected. This was no long and slender, shiny, silver cassette for hiding money, or perhaps paper. Shiny and silver, yes, but skinny? No. It was perhaps two feet deep and rolled out across the tile floor smoothly from its metal shelving.

As the lid unlatched and lifted, he smelled the contents within before he saw them ... leather. Leather-bound books and a few chips of wood, like piano keys, burned with foreign symbols or lettering. The books and parchments—paper treasures—some more loosely held together than others, rested within, long forgotten.

A gasp escaped him as the undeniable weight of lifelong suppression was surfacing, begging to be lifted, if this was what Jesse thought it could be. Carefully now, reaching inside and cradling the uppermost tome in his fingers and then lifting back the cover verified his deepest wish, for written in the fading corner was the name of his father—*James Bankole*.

XV

The Fall

Jesse had fallen off the wagon. It was the hardest fall he had ever experienced ... the final blow ... the end. It wasn't two weeks hence that he lay among the scattered journals of his father's memories. He lay there on the tile floor of the bank's vaulted room from noon to dusk rummaging through the contents of the safe deposit box. What was written in the books was nothing entirely so special, just the goings on of a man who was losing his memory and grasping to those empty pages with pen and ink as a last attempt at saving his treasured life. Though in the end, for Jesse had bore witness, he would inevitably lose his valued memories into the dark expanse of endless sea from whence they'd come.

The sight of these books did nothing but confirm to Jesse that keeping such chronological accounts was not worth the effort. He would rather spend *his* time in celebration and experience than waste it writing in a journal sure to be forgotten. On the other hand, these journals did confirm to him that he was not born alone. He had a *brother*, a twin unknown to him. It was only Jesse who was taken back and granted citizenship in America. Jesse could not determine the reason. But, it was not the books themselves that threw Jesse into a fit of despair, at first. It was the photo.

From among the age-stained tattered leaflets had fallen a black-and-white photo he recognized at once. The long sleek hair, the eyes expressing glittering emerald light, if that was possible to capture in black-and-white, and the lips. The lips a perfect fig.

It was Evelyn! But that, it could not be! This could not be Evelyn. These journals had aged with his father and surely this photo was older still! Catching his breath under the fading light that flooded into the open vault, he meticulously examined the picture and the book from whence it had emerged.

Not only had the sight of the photo been a blow to his psyche, but his constant struggle in repressing the thought of Evelyn, during the time of their separation, was nearly breached when he considered the possibility that the photograph had been one of his mother.

His father's eye for the same beauty only meant that Evelyn would have been yet an even more appropriate bride to his eternal soul than ever. Now, it couldn't just be a game to Jesse because the thought of losing, at this point, had become unbearable. Momentarily, he considered it a trick from God. A god who sat there laughing as he had come so close to capturing the heaven that he long sought but instead threw it all away in play. He managed however to push the threatening thought of mistake away in the fashion he had become so adept in doing and went back to examining the parchments.

In the absence of thoughts of loss, he allowed a warmth to grow alongside the relieving weight that had been lifted, because he now believed he had seen his mother. He even fancied that he might have known her for the brief time that he fell in love with Evelyn. He had then continued through his father's old belongings with a lighter heart, smiling.

Just when Jesse had reached the peak of pleasure and fulfillment on his temporary quest, but had not yet turned his focus to the future reunion with his love, is when it all came tumbling down … hard.

It was as if the Devil had swept away a foundation of the very Earth on which he stood and let the mountains crumble down upon him while he plummeted.

It was to these depths he would fall in confusion after finding the one simple thing that never should have sat among the relics of his father's.

It was the map. A map of Western Africa and a focused twisting trail though rugged jungle to a place so boldly marked … **Oxychana Tribe**.

***

The contents of the box had been piled back inside in a state of disarray and the map and picture left the bank with Jesse. The man’s mind was currently drawn blank and only one thing he could think of might take off the edge … the bar. The closest bar, Spinsters, had been but a short jog across the street and two blocks down, but it had been busy, so Jesse kept on running. The one thing on his mind as he breathed steadily in-and-out now was a drink. A drink and silence.

The key bearing the complacent twenty-two had now been pocketed and the documents he folded neatly into a front pocket of his (thankfully) high-end sweat suit. Here, they would be safe if he began to sweat ... and sweat he did, profusely. The casual drinking, which was deemed okay to him by belief, now fought against him as he pumped, pulsing from the pores in his skin initially meant to take in nutrients, not expel toxins, but this was how it was.

Then … there … he saw it, the place he needed to be in this very moment to keep himself from going mad or dying from exhaustion, whichever came first. A wooden table cloaked in shadow, set deep back in the recess of a hole-in-the-wall downstairs bar. He slowed to a quick walk and tried to steady his breath so he would not look like a lunatic, sweating his ass off, while ordering a stiff drink.

Though New York was riddled with ladies in spandex tights and sweatbands, the thought of judgmental insanity would only further send him into coincidental déjà vu and madness. So he forced himself to breathe, and then he forced himself to assume the most natural look possible as if he fit in among the scheme of things.

'No one cares, here, no one sees me freaking out,' he thought, as he slowly let himself find the chair within the shadowy alcove.

'Whew,' he thought, in conjunction to the waitress' audible greeting.

"That's a nice sweat suit! I see it's keeping you warm in this cold weather." She had said this playfully, while offering a tray teeming with tumblers of liquor.

Jesse pounded two of them straight down, disregarding the face of the hostess and hardly recognizing the burning cinnamon sensation that followed in his chest.

What he ordered from the waitress escaped him as he pulled the map out and spread it wide across the table. He dug in the left-hand pocket of his windbreaker pulling out a soft pack of Marlboro cigarettes and shook one to the top, pinching the filter in his lip and drawing it out of the red and white packaging. A quick flick and it was lit.

Smoke now swirled upward in the dim section of the bar, where he sat hovering over this old map, which was not entirely complete, for that plot of land had been inhabited and graded out for tourism some fifteen years ago. The map he'd bought for Evelyn taught him that much. If he had never purchased that map in Greece for her, he may not have recognized the jagged piece of land that the document portrayed, but he *had* purchased it. He had gotten it as a gift for her and slowly marked the now not-so-natural trail to her homeland; and yes, he had even put a time.

With a hand upon the spot of map that bore Evelyn's tribal name, he fell back into his chair, surrendering his weight to it. His heavy weight, which had only been momentarily lifted from his shoulders only hours before, and now was returning to him slowly in an entirely different manner. It was very different, this weight, not so much as trying to force a lie, but an unwillingness to accept a mountain of horrifying truth.

What did this mean, this picture of his mother? Was she an Oxychana? It was then he let the questions flood every nook and cranny of his mind, overwhelming him to the point that he hadn't noticed the waitress refilling his mug time and time again.

In his thoughts, he swam as a fish chasing its dinner in the sea and other times he was the one who ran from the threatening predators that inhabited that now bountiful water of his consciousness. Was his father's memory only so bad because of the practices of Oxychana spirit flight? Had his father participated in these ceremonies at all? Hell, his father might have even been a suitor sent to Evelyn herself, but no, he was much too old for that. Could his father have been a suitor for Evelyn's mother?! No! No! He screamed in response to the empty recess of his mind where no one waited to answer.

"No! I will not think it!"

He had screamed aloud from his shadowy corner, now littered with empty mugs and tumblers, not aware of the hushed reaction of those in earshot; not aware of the bartender telling the waitress to see him out. Not caring if they saw him now for who he was.

'I am a drunkard, that is what they see, and that is a more than ample disguise for me,' he thought as he stepped out into the cold.

He pulled his hood taut over his head and buried his trembling hands deep in his pockets.

'As long as they don't see what is going on inside my head,' he thought, as he walked the slippery streets of the Big Apple.

XVI

Returning Home

"I'm with child."

Evelyn knew it for sure only a moment after pulling open the accordion-style leather envelope he had left behind for her.

Though, the first time he had been the gentleman, and been careful, the encounters ever since were of love, deep passionate love with no regrets or doubts ... and there were no precautions taken.

All in all, she had expected *something* from him, perhaps a proposal to re-ignite their dedication to one another after his *gift*, as he called it (of the girls). But she had never expected him to disappear entirely. She had never met this man's equal. Admitting that to herself was easy. Sure, she used a bit of the time he had given her to enjoy the company of her new friends, though she had endured (for weeks on end) their apologies that he had gone.

The three girls had pampered her and loved her as if she had lost her mother to the darkness, as though it was their duty to be her saviors from misery. She lavished in it for a time. But inside her womb she carried him. Five months, which was the date he had marked for her return home, had started out okay, but now her back was aching with the extra weight of the ever-growing life within her.

Greg had agreed to accompany Evelyn to the residential community which had replaced Mohammed's military installment after all those years. It was there that she could find the trail which had been laid before her to the village.

She never lay with Greg, though his warm and friendly glances beckoned her from time to time. He was a gentleman, and in many ways he reminded her of Jesse; for that she was grateful. But she *loved* Jesse, and though he permitted her to lay with Emily it would not be the same for her with other *men*.

She prayed nightly that he had found his father and made amends and hoped that the dated map meant that they would meet again. Wishing he were here to hold her hand along the way, she settled instead for a group of teenage women held up in a shelter, that oddly resembled half of an abandoned interstate bridge. The residential community was merely a collection of poorly-built houses scattered sparsely among an approximate ten-block section of cleared-away forest. And the road they had come in on, since the outskirts of Owerre, had been a single lane consisting of poorly-poured blacktop.

Being there in Africa was euphoric to her. Using the old French was at first oddly awkward, but it began coming easier to her. Heck,

Evelyn had spoken mostly English for so long, she thought in it. She fancied that even her dreams were woven English, and that is when she'd known the full transition had been made.

It was ironic to be translating her native language into English at first until she got the hang of it again. But being amongst the women there, who would have been taken as street rats back in London or Greece, she found herself acting in a more natural way.

Here, they were merely people working together and living together by different means. Here, the community was much closer knit, because it *had* to be. Perhaps these ladies even slept in those houses when they were not over-crowded, or maybe they even rotated shifts. She didn't let the question capture her. However, it was growing dark and neither did she want to stay in such a foreign place for the night. She wanted to be down the trail and into her old village before the darkness completely enveloped them.

A child had been sent ahead to alert the village of their presence, and she had kissed Greg who had been so helpful and loving to her since Jesse had departed. She pleaded with him to leave her to her fate on this trail, and he fought with skillful verbiage, arguing that he would accompany her, or at least wait here for her, but she would not have it. Evelyn couldn't see him staying in a place like this overnight. For what she knew, he was alien to this type of living. At least *she* knew what she was getting herself into and she felt welcome among the people. When he left, she knew he would find a place in Owerre where he could keep a vigil for a few days, just in case she came back empty-handed.

The village was there. Evelyn knew from the way they had spoken about the dealings in Oxychana root. The ancient herb had been recently traded with the people here for plastic jugs and modern clothing. PVC piping had been carried and exchanged, among other goods, for the sweet fruits her mother used to grow in the fertile soil within. She felt that her mother grew them still.

The grading machines that had leveled this section of land, leading to the trail, must have brought in drier clay, and left behind cement and gravel building remains.

After leaving the small community in the company of her female escorts, it baffled her how the contrast was quickly changing. While crossing a small wooden bridge, not more than a plank, she thought how the feel in the community likened to an Arizona parking lot surrounded by ominously ensuing jungle. She almost expected to hear the big machines still working their hydraulics as they moved. That was what it reminded her of—a construction site that had not been finished. However, now that they had walked the small wooden bridge, which served to make an easier transition from the rubble of the site, to the floor of the jungle, she was thrust into her past.

The trail opened up to a well-worn path that one would have missed if not directed by the locals to it. Thin metal posts held a low rope that drooped its way along either side of the walkway. A copper lamp accented well-placed wooden poles after every hundred yards or so, and they were not alone for the entirety of the trek.

Twice they came upon a couple walking their direction, bound with baskets and sacks—no doubt headed back to what she'd had already coined 'the site'—and once upon the child who had sent their message, during his return.

She knew now, for certain, that her mother still resided among them. That certainty was not, however, the most notable part of the trek. Instead, the most euphoric thing she had encountered on the way was something which had only been mentioned in the oldest tales of all … it was the Dolmen.

The Dolmen sat receded in the Earth and chained off much like an exhibit. The dark abyss that was its interior could be made out from under the lip of smooth rock that somehow tricked the eyes into thinking it was nothing but an outcropping.

"There is a cavern there … I know it … I see it … I feel it," she thought passing beside it.

Much like a picture puzzle tricks the mind and finally you realize you can see a pretty young lady *and* a crone by simply shifting your perception; the Dolmen spoke to her. She could see the cavern; she could see the trick the eyes were playing on her mind, and the way the stone of the Dolmen gently helped its allure. But could anyone else see the blackness of that cave? She didn't know and she had not asked, but she did inquire of the plaque that resided at the forefront of the grayish, stony megalith. It bore three questions:

Who but I can let known the secrets of the unhewn dolmen?
Who but I can make known the ages of the moon?
Who but I can find the secret resting place of the sun?

-Douglas Monroe

These questions presented themselves as a cool sensation at her wrist, and the sensation—bringing her attention to her moon-shaped charm—had her thinking of Jesse, off on his own adventure while she listened to the Njaran woman's recollection of current events.

"An American archeologist, and a company of journalists, brought all of this here."

"An American?"

"Yes. Many writers and researchers visited over the course of two years. This once insignificant spot, they made a point to protect while Obasanjo built North of the river. The resident researchers found artifacts tying the Dolmen, and other standing stones near, to the subterranean world of South Africa, which is largely known as one of the wealthiest provinces on Earth.

"Man's conquest for gold," she had said, "stains even the most sacred places untouched. However, the village had protection under Obasanjo and the relative sensitivity that they practiced while they did their research was noble enough. The resources it brought through the years were an agreeable exchange as far as the populated region is concerned not far North of here. The village children still spread rumor that beneath us may be the final resting place of King Arthur."

The name brought Evelyn back fully back to the jungle, "It has been so long since I have heard such legends. I knew the era had pressed in on us from outside, but to have gotten so close? Are such things only legends to *you,* Njaran?"

The woman turned, sticking the end of her staff into the soft mud along the trail's edge, "Sometimes—"

Now everything was coming together for Evelyn. Obasanjo and Mohammed must have gone forward with their plans of the Northern community, and she felt indebted to him for keeping his word and leaving the South untouched, but the proximity to local libraries had waned the beliefs along the outskirts of Oxychana.

"—I wish that a man would make a decision for me to stay or leave, so I could pick a side. The Mantle of Arthur may hide his remains, after emerging here following the battle of the trees. My children seem to say it is so. The blood runs in my veins, dear lady, but opportunity is all that I can offer my offspring today. Opportunity seems to exist more out there, than under the canopy anymore." The guide then turned the back of her head and continued on—the tightly woven rows of hair bobbing in parallel lines behind her.

A bench offered the weary traveler a spot to rest from where they departed into a thicker swath of jungle. If the area around the Dolmen had been opened to the public, a child may become subject to the dangerous pitfall beyond the barrier which was disguised beneath solid granite. The thought troubled her. But her happiness and reverence, as one who was part of these mysteries by blood, outweighed any disturbing thoughts she may have had.

Fruits were now growing abundantly along the trail and the smell of Oxychana already had begun welcoming her into its embrace. The closer she came strengthened her urge to fly with her mom again on invisible wings. It would not be long until she was in Mom's embrace and she had accepted that she would be here *regardless* of Jesse's actions, for hadn't she told herself, many years ago, as she loved Adam, that if she were to bear a child … she would return?

XVII

The Flight

Thoughts of an ocean's purple hue, touched by pinkish cloudy skies, rode with Evelyn as she sat with her mother in the dugout bowl of her abode. The snug little hut that her mother now had to herself was packed with purple pillows and lacy things that she adored. A tiny, tiled kitchenette had been built here with ready water from the spring, brought along through PVC hidden in the earth, where their house had stood so long ago.

It was a modern, cleanly-kept lodge within, set right out in the middle of a hidden village. The other villagers had houses which were built in much the same fashion, but none of them were this luxurious. Straw and dry palm roofing cones still prevailed, but more prominent building material was in the walls.

It was nighttime when she'd arrived, and the people had all been inside their homes with candle-lamps burning among the welcoming sounds of the surrounding forest and comforting night-cap of the canopy. It was different, but it was home. And the feeling that she had of dread had slowly faded with the aroma and ever-present smoke of the Oxychana.

Her mother had embraced her warmly with a smile and a teary-eyed thankfulness, which could not be faked. Though the practices of the Oxychana had not changed nor had their beliefs, her mother had become lonely after her father had passed away. She could never know for sure if he was truly dead, but he had been gone two years and no word had come.

Evelyn offered comfort in the only way she knew how, by giving the details of her own story since she fled with Adam, while her mother sat quietly and listened as she smoked the dried and rolled herb she knew too well. But it was not until she took the small Quid from her mother and tucked it into her cheek in a simple, automatic fashion that her mom opened up to her the secrets she had been keeping buried all this time.

The potent sour liquid of the bundled roll of leaf didn't begin seeping into the sensitive porous flesh of her gums until long after her mother had explained the reason for her father's lengthy absences of her youth. She had told her of the responsibility that had been passed down to her through generations.

Evelyn had never been given the opportunity to grow close to her grandmother, who died when she was but a toddler, but she had also been a Seeker. This practice had been a search that began countless ages ago and the stories had been forbidden of ever being committed to writ. It had been for this reason that underground cellars housed long stretches of twine where leaves had been strung sequentially together, as if to be flipped through one by one while walking along the lines.

Evelyn had left before being extensively schooled in the totem writing, but she had known that it existed. She had walked the lines of leaves flipping, accompanied by her father, seeing all the different symbols of intricate lines which had been burned into the surface of each. Each one represented a letter or phrase, the meaning that only those of the purest tribal blood would ever know. It was only in this way that their most sacred teachings could be passed down and documented without violating the religious laws.

Her mother never faltered, only sat with glassy eyes that looked reminiscent of old, as she revealed the truth about Evelyn's *real* father.

The fluids from the pack of herb now settled in Evelyn's cheek and she felt the onset ensuing of the trance. She reached into her gums and hooked the mashy substance in her mouth with two fingers, hoping to stop the effects from taking hold. She slung it to the ground in hazy anger, meaning to shout out at her mother in disbelief, but it was too late.

The flight had begun, any moment she knew she would be standing along those seas of purple with her mom, and there would be nowhere or no want to run away.

Her mom, who had witnessed the reaction, not unexpectedly, bid her sit awhile before the flight had taken them fully. There was more to tell, and she needed know it to guarantee the direction of the flight.

It was the question which had forced Evelyn to run away, really. The voice inside that argued with the practice of her people, the question that always was with her, but that she had never voiced. And it was now that her mother summoned the question, by beckoning it from her, to the room.

"Did you not ask yourself, my daughter? The same thing I asked myself before defying the pact that was our upbringing?"

Evelyn looked to her, her mind sharpening for a moment in pure intent, and in a split second of understanding she realized that her mother had defied the pact as well.

“Who is the man of the Sun? And how will I know?” The question came from Evelyn as perfect melody sings from the clarinet of a woodwind master.

It was in this moment that her mother leaned in to embrace her, "I met him in the forest, halfway to Owerre." Then whispering through the silken hair that hung as a curtain before Evelyn's ear, “A white man. A Welsh of Anglo-Saxon blood. And Like you, I had suitors which Grandmother turned away. Like you, I questioned if I could make the choice while under the influence of the Oxychana leaf.”

Evelyn leaned back gently to see square into her mother's eyes who still gripped her arms with weathered fingers, attempting to keep her daughter's focus here in the moment.

“This white man was my father?”

“Yes,” Her mother said softly. “James was an adventurer. He would travel from the city nightly, and trekked through the lushness of vine and leaf and inner wood to the Dolmen. It was where we met and coupled. He had a map to find the Dolmen and I had marked for him the location of our tribe with the red tincture of the burlap berry that grew generously then. Of course, back then it was but a jagged point of stone, but it was magical." Then with question in her voice, "Oh, Evelyn. You must have doubted your relationship to Elithis—your godfather—at some time.”

Evelyn didn’t know how to respond. The question had never come, for that part of her life had been left behind as surely as Jesse had left her behind in Greece.

She was succumbing to the flight and yet her mother’s eyes still held firm. She imagined that she heard something said about Elithis being too dark to have conceived a child with such pale skin, before she let herself fall comfortably back against the abundant softness of those purple pillows, and then could do nothing more but listen, and dream.

Her mother’s words then came alive as she received them, twisting and dancing among paisley colored drifts of wind and smoke; each word a cliff on which to hang and each phrase a moral in itself. But she heard her speaking, slowly speaking, sometimes in rhyme, of the horror of being taken by her suitor after knowing she was already full with babe. The way she loved Elithis in a different way than she had held James. She explained that Elithis knew that Evelyn was not his own, and this is why he was permitted to leave on journey. It was his duty, in a way, to find a suitable partner in which to plant his seed, and it was his right.

"Also, it was his job alone to send the suitors for you at my request. And when you disappeared and Serat came hurrying to my hut, I knew that you had found the one. It was with a heavy heart that we managed our way to the very spot you'd disappeared, and I could only make half the trek. Serat returned with no word of you and I knew you all too well. I can only guess it is his babe you carry now within you. Like mother, like daughter I suppose ..."

With those words, the old lady settled back herself, flying to her daughter who would be waiting on the shores of Pangea.

But she had guessed wrong.

Standing on the shores of Pangea, in the dream-state of the Oxychana, was something Evelyn had not done since she was but a teenager. Now, she stood alongside her mother, not as her pupil, but as her equal. They each gazed out across the seas, from which their beliefs say that they had come. Mohami's beliefs anyway.

Evelyn had not the slightest clue, now, what she believed down deep and true. She remembered the story of Man's creation from the Bible, and found it lovely. She fancied the way that the first couple had lived in perfect union and stood naked with no shame. She did not, however, fully understand why forbidden fruit would have ever played a part. If she had found herself among such a paradise with the one she loved, would she ever need anything more? She could not answer.

In this state of mind, there were no problems. She could hear the thoughts of her mother just as clearly as if she had watched the words purse from her lips themselves. She could see that her mother assumed the baby in her womb was Adam's (the man in the jungle whom she had met). And along with that assumption she knew also that the thought of her bearing another Seeker for the tribe was in her mother's mind. The thought occurred to her within these mists of vivid dreams and was not at all terrifying to her, yet the thought would surely send her running had she not been under the influence of the ancient herb.

She would not tell her mother that really, she was nothing like her. Not here, not now, anyway. She was, for a time unknowingly and undoubtedly under her mother's solid charm. She had not mentioned Jesse to her, and the bracelet bearing her symbolic eternal connection to him had obviously seemed little more than a trinket. Though Evelyn was somehow under her mother's vague enchantment, she treasured the thoughts of Jesse which still were secret in her mind.

If not for the initial realization that her mother saw fit to raise her baby as Oxychana, she may not have put up the mental barrier which was crucial in assuring that she would not surrender her precious secret. Her mother wasn't looking for another man among the tale, so that made it more likely that she would not venture into Evelyn's thoughts deep enough to dredge it from her mind. She always thought of her mother as supernaturally cunning, a notable strength, but Evelyn would take advantage of the single weakness she still possessed … her vanity.

The flight was entirely one-sided. She held her mother's hand and listened to the thoughts come through as they rose above the breaking waves and drifted as a downy feather in the wind, around and over the lush forest with its emerald foliage and lucid burning fruits of red, in abundance. They rose higher as if they were an eagle catching the spiraling updraft in its massive wings. Above the Super Continent, they flew inward toward its center, where the massive volcano, which reached infinitely upward towards the heavens, produced warm torrents of steamy thermals catching the wings that were their souls. Twisting up around the massive peak of the still smoldering magma within, they rushed upward in the pure white steam that was their Mother Earth's first breath of life.

When Evelyn made out patterns in the smoky whiteness of the flight, she knew that she was coming to. It wasn't a struggle, she simply let life come back to her at its leisure. When her eyes once again regained some focus and her skin picked up on the gentle strokes of chilly paint that was being applied to her, she breathed in deeply as if trying to regain possession of her soul from the very air around her.

The scents of the hut reminded her instantly of where she was, the sandalwood and myrrh, and of course, the Oxychana. She was safe, and her left hand traveled slowly from the arm of the wicker chair in which she had been placed—while she was unconscious, she guessed—to the slight roundness of her belly, which now was decorated with the spiral of the invocation. The warmth of the life within her permeated the skin of her tummy and moved into her hand, and she smiled. She saw her mom working at the fireplace, which had been mortared up with stone, a small chimney breaching the lofty rooftop. A cauldron hung within the interior and fresh spices were orderly atop the table to the left. Evelyn remembered that this was a sure sign of festival in this small commune, and saw flecks of the bluish paint along the arms of mother as she worked.

She was here, at the spot marked on the map that she had followed, and she had no map to where she was going next, nor ever considered it. Suddenly confused and directionless, Evelyn began to accept the possibility that this *was* home.

XVIII

X Marks the Spot

If nothing else, Jesse is an extremist. Whether, due to the events that drove him there, or if it is only hereditary he does not know. He does not know but he lives it, because it is a fact. He loves deeply, and he feels losses deeply. He never hates, it isn't in him. However, if he did, it would be a tyrannical kind of hate, a heated hatred that would draw followers blindly to their hells. It is always this way with him, pouring himself into everything passionately with no regard of his own loss at all. If it is his conscious actions that trained his automated bodily responses to this same breakneck pace, it can't be told, but when the neuro-degenerative illness took hold it did so with the same devastatingly brutal speed. But Jesse had been raised of strong blood, an adventurer's blood, mixed with a tribal mother's blood in which magic flowed.

A doctor would have stopped him sooner, but Reverend Williams was no doctor. At first, he only offered a listening ear to the well-kept, obviously intoxicated, man, but on the third day of confession he had prepared something for him.

It wasn't the first time he had heard the confessions of incest, but the one other time had been so brief and but a selfish act of burying one's guilt. This man, however, seemed confused and today he seemed troubled. He was having a hard time with his memory. He still knew that his act was unintentional, and maybe even unconfirmed, but Williams heard absolution in his voice more often than not.

Absolution. The one thing a holy man does his job for. Absolution was at hand for Reverend Williams, for on the opposing side of the screen was his path to it.

"Forgive me father, for I have sinned."

"This is the third day, my son. You said your Hail Marys?"

"Yes."

"Then you are cleansed," Williams whispered through lips crossed in deliberation.

The Reverend couldn't fight back the memory of the face which was black and slick, with eyes that burned as cinders at their rings. The Dark Angel who had beckoned him at his time of reckoning to educate the incestuous on the many teachings of the Biblical beginnings of Adam and Eve; the face threatened him, yet comforted him. There was no absolution for this Reverend save through the Dark Angel, now. Yet the Angel offered him peace. And he was weary of it all. 'Let it be done.'

"There is no further need to beat yourself up over this my son. I am here to listen, that is all." Then with secret self-indulgence added, "But if you need some guidance, I would surely meet with you tonight, if you'd accept my counsel."

Jesse traced the figure of the sun that hung around his neck and found himself lost in confusion. Was he wounded in the jungle? Did he sit with cocoa and speak with Evelyn about the Bible? He had been bingeing, and the neuro-degenerative illness had utilized this weakness to drive in deep and take hold. He would not forget her, never forget *her*. His memories were nothing compared to the ones they shared together. If anything would be allowed to get caught, on the drifting winds of forgetfulness it would be those he offered first—his.

Those winds *would* come, howling through his mind and taking with them every visual memory not burned deep down inside, but not now. And when they came, he would be prepared. He had his map, at least. But today he *did* need guidance. There were but two weeks until the date was up, the date he had marked boldly on his own map one night in a drunken stupor, just as he had done on Evelyn's.

He thought to forget everything he knew *could* end up a blessing, if they met again. But he was here, trying to make amends with whatever God he still knew. Before his God, he wanted to lay it out like a naked babe held up in the light. He wanted to be judged before he went into the future that he knew was unforgiving. He knew that once the disease had him for good, that he would not know what had befallen him here. He would not remember that she and he were of a single blood.

He wouldn't remember those things because he would never let them live within him. This was for sure because he didn't burn those thoughts into his head, instead he fought them. He fought them not by resistance, but by pure unacknowledgement. He would drink and run and take a thumb of powder to his nose if it was readily available, anything to keep moving and doing, so he'd not have time to think or dwell on the reality of the sin he would eventually commit again, if she would have him.

But that had run its course and he couldn't torture his own body with such efforts anymore. He needed something to focus on as the time ticked away, something to be engulfed in so that his mind wouldn't go back to that vault and those journals. All he needed, he had with him: the map, the picture, and the amulet that was his link to her. All he lacked was the ability to jump forward in time two weeks and already be on a plane or in a jungle.

But he must settle for this, this pastor's offer of guidance. Perhaps the Adam of the Bible, or was it *him*—for now he'd grown unsure—held an answer so dear he could find resolve. So as the icy winds howled among the New York salted streets and the gargoyles offered stony gazes from the rooftop of the church, he listened.

It was a sobering time for Jesse to sit with Reverend Williams on a daily basis. The Reverend found Jesse attractive and very cunning. It had been obvious that his memory was bust, for Jesse was an open man and offered his story uncensored all the way. The things the Reverend told him he found some comfort in. He liked the way the man pointed out to him that, at one point, everyone was united as a people.

"The world of man spoke but one language before the building of the Tower of Babel," he would say, "but on the day that God saw that man was not ready for ultimate knowledge the tower had been struck down, and the languages of man had been separated and incoherent to one another.

"God saw that man, existing with one language and all intelligence, would come together and try and build a tower to heaven, which contained the ultimate knowledge. As simple men, united as they were, they built.

"They had built for centuries the huge tower to the heavens, convinced that when they touched it they would know the *ultimate* truths. The tower went up in steps like the great pyramids of Egypt, and from every corner of the world people brought brick and mortar to achieve this feat. But when it was complete, God was unsatisfied. And so it goes he had gifted man with knowledge and abundance, but man had been too young and in his ignorance had sought the one thing that he had already possessed, in turn wasting his precious moments in desire rather than offering them up to God in thanks. In the end, God had cast it down.

"A lesson to mankind to be thankful for every moment, and this is why I praise him everyday, Jesse." The Reverend said this while resting a gentle hand upon his shoulder.

Jesse saw something in those eyes that was troubling him, it was as if they searched for something in his own eyes. He would briefly question why the man would look at him in a manner such as this, a manner akin to asking outside a door ... 'Is anybody home?'

'I'm here,' he thinks immediately and brushes the feeling off as if it was another one of his memories going out the door. But then he *does* ask, "Reverend, is this all fact? Does the tower really exist? If so, wouldn't someone have found proof of such a massive endeavor?"

He had been recently encompassing himself with oddities of mind and the Reverend, his friend, was always willing to humor him in such exchanges.

"Indeed. I'm sure there have been many expeditions to find such a place. The Bruner Family Historians have long thought the Great Pyramid of Giza to be remnant of man's early attempt to touch the sky and see God. But, Bruner Egyptology is a cult of sorts themselves, very secretive." The Reverend's brow furled with a bit of worry, detectable only for a second while his gaze broke away momentarily.

"So ... there are those who *do* believe?" Jesse's mind is more weary than ever.

Evelyn's frequent stories were coming to the apex of his thoughts. He could hear her voice all over again, and see her flying over the Great Pyramid upon Pangea during her spirit training. Clearly he could recall the documentation in his father's portfolios; *The location of the tribe in reference to the Giza Plateau could make it possible that the Bruners have it right.*

"The strength of God's will is unimaginable," answered Williams, "Jesse"—there was that look again—"with but the faith of a mustard seed, you can move mountains."

Shrugging the man's hand from his shoulder Jesse almost hears a click as a puzzle piece falls into place in his mind. His thoughts were so involved with the coincidence and his eyes averted as to break that questionable stare, that he hardly felt the hand of Reverend Williams sliding down the inside of his thigh and gently grabbing bundled sweat pants where there might have been his penis. The man had moved closer to him now and Jesse felt an awkwardness he'd never known.

"You're alone, Jesse."

The voice sickened him when it came, and brimming on the hazard that was his hatred-never-breached, he pushed himself away in anger and humility.

"What, did you think you could just cop a feel because eventually I won't remember?!" Jesse lashed out, the Reverend now standing still as stone and looking on in sympathy as if *he* were the one in need of comfort.

"You're sick, Jesse. You need help." A slightly wrinkled hand out in offering, those wrinkles Jesse had not noticed until now.

Perception, even now, played such a role with things and this is something he knew for sure. Before, this man was gentle, helpful, caring, and he had envisioned him five years lesser in his youth. But now with his revealed intent, the flaws that weren't there before were vivid and acute. He makes a mental note that is his best tool, mayhap his only tool, to see the hidden image from now on, to never get caught unaware of things right out in front of him again. The old man, now exposed, looked ten years older, and Jesse felt nothing but pity for the fool that he was and so turned away and left the man to wallow in his shame.

The time was close now and Jesse had his weapon. The Reverend might have been a pervert or a lonely fool amiss of a pretty face, which Jesse surely had, but he had provided Jesse with the one thing that could make him look ahead, renewed faith. Faith, not in people, the Reverend had surely destroyed what little bit of that which did remain, but faith in himself.

He had no father anymore, no one to judge him but he alone. What was right and wrong was his to decide and the twisted Reverend had said it best amongst his tales, "*We all came from the Adam and of the Eve, and thus all were at one time a single blood, held protected and right in the eyes of God.*"

He also knew that if fate had dealt him such a blow, then he would strike back with one of his own. If it took even resurrecting the Tower of Babel itself, then so be it.

The faith of but a mustard seed *could* move mountains, and this *was* a belief that he would burn for hours into his depths and test as he found his way to the trail marked so boldly on the map in his possession.

The same map, only a few hours after his flight's departure, would be little more than a marker for his malfunctioning memory.

Jesse stared at the woman in the black and white photo that occupied his grip and recalled her advice.

"Memories need markers," she had once said.

That advice had him chanting to himself quietly while the airplane occupied the airs over the Atlantic, "This woman, this place. This woman, this place. This woman, this place."

… and just one more in-flight cocktail would bring him safely in.

XIX

Serat

Serat had grown into a handsomely chiseled man of Africa. His skin was smooth and dry, and the muscle tone more prominent than any other tribesman. He normally wore the modern cut-off shorts and tank-tops brought from the site, but today he wore his tribal quilt-like bachran that showed the cuts of muscle in his sturdy legs, and left his chest bare, save the string of wooded tree nuts he'd collected in the past. His foot gripped the edge of the counter by the chair where Evelyn sat. His foot now covered in these thin suede shoes that bore the symbol of a leaping puma, clean and new… and expensive.

Evelyn, she was so beautiful. She had matured, and being with babe only made her shine more in his eyes. She had not recognized him yet. He had been applying the ceremonial paint that was prepared while she had been flying. He knew that she was to bear the next Seeker, and that she would need a man to partner as her satellite into the world for her child's suitors if it were female. He remembered her well, and had missed her from the day she had been taken. His first instinct was to kill the man that had stolen her away from him so long ago, but the man that had arrived here wasn't the white man that he remembered.

It was just afternoon when the blue-eyed man had appeared, confused. The man bore a map that marked the tribe's location, and Serat immediately knew that it was old. It was a reproduction of the surrounding area back at the time of her disappearance, before the site had started building. The thought that the blue-eyed man could ever possibly have anything to do with his beloved Evelyn wasn't fully apparent until he had seen the photo of Mohami, her mother. They struck such a resemblance that one could easily be mistaken for the other. Serat had sat with him in his hut, as Evelyn, only yards away, dreamed away her day amongst her past.

***

Jesse's French was something that his mind had not cast out. Languages were something that stuck with him. It had something to do with body language, he would think to himself. People all make the same gestures; it is only in the notes and chords that tempo strikes the changes. He did well among many cultures in his travels, but here now, he was a knowledgeable man, but one without a memory.

Only the **X** on his map had served as an obvious goal and the picture in his pocket served as the driving force behind it. Both of these he had handed to the Oxychana man who now gladly shared with him the odd smelling cigarette from which he pulled deep long drags.

Jesse had offered him a Marlboro in return but the man denied it. He did, however, notice that Serat—that was his name, he thought—was particularly interested in his Pumas. Jesse always loved the feel of Puma tennis shoes. They were so light and non-obstructive to his steady gait. He noticed the man's interest in them and thought to use it as a card.

Also he saw that Serat was overly shocked at seeing the amulet he possessed. *A rare jewel that was meant to reunite his people*. Serat was adamant about the legend through the day, and Jesse began to feel a bit euphoric from the smoking herb inside the abode. But he wanted, no *needed*, to know about this amulet. It was one of the three things that were anything to him anymore, as far as he remembered.

Serat knew exactly what he wanted. He also knew exactly how to get it. Ever since the message boy had brought word that Evelyn had returned, he felt the fires of his passion re-ignite the blazes that would melt that solid block of ice that was his heart. Since she had gone his insides had been empty, hollow, sleeping, and upon her return every internal piece of him now stirred in such a wakeful dance, it was as if a battery had been popped into a child's mechanical toy that lay long forgotten.

Mohami had immediately summoned Serat to make the preparations, for if her visions held true—and her sight had never failed her—Evelyn would be ceremonially received by him in the coming morn. He knew one thing was for certain. He would say anything to keep another man from taking his life force from him once again. It was a tangled web that Serat had been weaving in Jesse's mind, to make sure what was his would not be lost again.

"What of the picture?" Jesse asks Serat. "Do you not recognize the lady there?"

"Sadly, she was my mother," said Serat, looking down at the black-and-white picture, as if very fond of it. "She passed during the Civil War many years ago. There is not a single photograph remaining of her today, save this one. If it would not be too much to ask, could I keep it?"

"If what you say is true, by all means it is yours." Jesse scoured Serat's expression looking for any sign of falsehood there, but could find none.

“Besides, you have returned, and with amulet in hand," Serat’s voice now suddenly filled with excitement, secretly hoping to kindle the same emotion in Jesse. "You must surely be in desperate need of seeing your journey to completion.”

His words had the desired effect.

After his long absence in the states, Jesse had been driven by nothing more than fleeting memories. His long primal desire for adventure had turned his sacred promises to ghosts, which he grasped at in the dark. The withdrawals—and now a touch of the Oxychana sage—had succeeded in rending his mind into total oblivion.

“I passed by this Dolmen, of which you speak, along the lighted path here. It was hard to make out in the dark beneath the canopy at dawn. Tell me more about this amulet. Please"—and still he grasped at smoke—"it is one of the few possessions that I hold dear. To it I am bound like nothing I have ever felt before. You say it is a relic of your tribe, but I‘m reluctant to part with it. Perhaps we can make an arrangement?”

Serat sat in thought for a moment, turning the picture of Mohami in his hand. He glanced now at the shoes on Jesse’s feet striving not to be too forward less he give away his ambitions.

“I have access to the key that unlocks the chained-off barrier of the Dolmen. Legend claims that within lie treasures beyond the imagination of mankind. Jewels and gold have little value to people such as we, yet only he who possesses the amulet can enter there. The entrance remains dormant to those without it. It is the space within which myth says tunnels deep within the confines of the Earth, and this is what is valued by our people. For only on the Sabbath days is light retold to permeate its interior, and here we would worship if the entrance could only be hewn open.

"Tomorrow is a ceremony of the people, of which I must attend and the village will be occupied, at which time you could go, with amulet in hand, and breach the shell. You would have time to take from within whatever treasures you wish." He perceived a spark of interest there, "I would ask only that you leave the relic behind and the entrance open to us. I have not offered this to even the archaeologists that funded current trade among our tribe." Serat conformed his expression to show a bit of uncertainty. Then he lightened and made to complete the transaction, "It seems you hold a key that would benefit me, and I one that would benefit you. Neither of import without the other."

Blasphemous as Serat thought the act may be, if he could only turn this man away, forever would he rest assured Evelyn would be by his side. Jesse may loot the cavern, if anything did exist within, but he could never gain entrance to the most sacred interior of its caves because he only possessed half of the known relic. The other half had been hanging from Evelyn's wrist as she lay unconscious in Mohami's tent.

Serat thought he had spied it when he'd heard of her return. A closer glance and he could verify it certainly, and already he considered her half among his own possessions.

When Jesse's arrival had been announced, Mohami and Evelyn were already deep into their flight and Serat was intrinsically charged with the protection of their Chieftain as she slept. The opportunity to receive him unbeknownst to them was mere coincidence. Now, this man's confounded memory served Serat, and the tiny bit of luck perhaps could rid him of this small annoyance before he was summoned to Mohami's hut again, upon her waking.

Jesse was weary, he had not slept at all this night. Between the strange thick scent that floated in the air, and now the heavy smoke settling in his lungs, his mind was swimming with a kind of nostalgic excitement at seeing what lay within this ancient unhewn chamber. Never had an adventure such as this, fallen into his lap, and now he was on the brink of an astounding exploration.

"How might I convince you to allow me the use of this key? Is a stranger's promise—to honor your wishes and leave the amulet behind—enough?"

"And the map, you must also promise to leave the map with me. Our Dolmen, I would not have over-run with outsiders and their commercial ways, as you have seen we remain hidden from the nearby cities, even trade is kept a secret by the local Njarans. I assume you will not have further need for it when you return there, if what you promise is honorable in nature."

With this, Jesse thought for awhile, considering returning to the Njaran village where his local escort was still waiting. They would take him back to Owerre and on to Nigeria when he returned. He thought he would need supplies of some fashion to venture into the catacombs, and what if there were treasures there, would he not need someone to help haul his bounty? He considered all the questions carefully and found that, much like the people here, he had no real need for riches. Of those, he had never been in short supply, and so, with reluctance, but still the same hazy excitement, he agreed.

The sun was now peeking through in thin gold rays, penetrating the uppermost of the green and moist above. Evening was creeping in, and Jesse was strangely intoxicated and on the brink of falling into sleep when Serat re-entered the hut and motioned him to the door. The key, which was a steel bolt of thick worn gray, two stumpy rods in blocky shapes protruding from a flat jeweled oval, and spun in golden fabric, hung with bluish tassels from his hand.

Serat, hurrying him out of the entrance by the small of his back, paused a moment before handing him the key, "You must go now. Straight up the trail will lead you home, and don't forget your noble promise."

He held the key out for Jesse to take but when he grasped it Serat held tight to it in resistance and Jesse looked one more time into his eyes.

"There is one more thing I ask, my friend." Serat said with cunning greed, and this Jesse immediately picked up on in his voice.

In question, he raised his eyebrows in response, secretly knowing what Serat was going to ask.

"Your shoes?"

The Ceremony

The painted spiral on Evelyn's tummy which twisted in and back around itself in a single unbroken line had dried to touch. Her mind was weary and her eyes possessed a strangely pleasant heaviness after the flight. She was being pampered here as if she had never left to begin with. It was comforting, and sleep had been the first thing on her mind until she had let her head fall sideways on the pillow, and spied the painting servant's familiarly covered foot. A shoe she knew too well. The black-and-white of the Pumas that this man wore were exactly the kind of shoe that Jesse had (not often, but sometimes) worn around the house in leisure. She just then began to think of the date that passed her by, with no sign of her love, and was to reach out for the map, which now lay among the bundle of her clothes, when she saw *him*.

Serat's eyes were on her like a falcon homing its kill in a deafening dive. The gleaming smile that opened slowly between his cheeks as recognition dawned on her was only overshadowed in perfection, by the broadness of his shoulders. In one hand, he held a wooden brush that had been applying the paint to her skin, and in his other was her hand. His fingers clasping just below the wrist where the moon he sought hung from silver loops, but he would not look to it yet, he was only aware of her.

She brought herself up to him and kissed him fully on the mouth in an act of exasperated, friendly, emotional reunion. This kiss Serat would hold a second longer than she'd meant, and the action had her mind raising questions that eventually must be answered. But he was very charismatic and he would intentionally rush his questions to her so that her mind would not fall victim to her doubts.

"Oh, how I've missed the sight of you, and you have grown into such a beautiful woman. I might have known! How do you feel?" He spoke with the upbeat joy and confidence that she remembered from his boyhood.

"I am a bit weary, but look at you! You are handsome, and a man! You've been eating."

"You know I couldn't stand to live on fruits and vegetable alone. Tilling in the drier weeks requires good meat, and I have learned to hunt. Perhaps, I should find a prize for you tonight, after you have rested."

Their hands still held one another as he spoke, and Mohami turned to them, resting the wooden ladle on its stem, "He has become quite the hunter and he is educated, too. I've had to pull him from the Totem Houses on many a morning just to make him eat. It is a surprise that he still has eyes to see you after straining them to read the leaves after the light has passed."

"You've deciphered the Totem language?" Evelyn asked him.

"Elithis had the Totem memorized well, I have merely learned it and set about reading them, and the stories that they hold are mesmerizing."

The smell of the stew, now bubbling hot within the cauldron, was overcoming any other. As Mohami served out deep cups of the gruel, Evelyn and Serat sat and reminisced about the past.

Eating brought a bit of life back to her. Her mind's eye, now thinking clearly, could picture Serat working to remove her dress and slip while she dreamed. He must have replaced her bra with this warm swath of beaded hide and fur, and she imagined his hands riding along the cup of her breast and the cut of her inner thighs as he tied her garments into place. They ate, and spoke, but she would never ask him if this were how it happened.

She thought of Greg and how she had denied him on more than one occasion. She thought briefly to herself that if Serat had beckoned her, she might not deny herself another pleasure. The time had passed, which had been marked so clearly on the map and, for the most part, Serat and her mother were keeping her in high spirits. They were keeping her happy, but in a way it was akin to coaxing an angry dog with a stinky piece of meat.

A servant girl entered the hut and retrieved the iron cauldron. Evelyn could see the scarred welts, deep markings in her shoulders under the thin veil of cloth around her neck and back. She watched as Serat's face grew cold and chiseled as she passed, and then Evelyn remembered the acts of Papa's servant guards and the brutal way they were lashed into subordination. *Memories suppressed for years, and actions that a child of the priest and priestess could only ignore*. The girl obediently and gracefully lifted the heavy pot, which was more a job for Serat than a thinning female. Nevertheless, she hauled it with humility out to the gardens where the ceremony was to be held.

Evelyn began to feel uneasy for the first time. She had been, of course, trying hard not to think of the what ifs but now she was forced to see the truth in what was happening. If Jesse did not come for her, she wondered if she would be able to leave here of her own free will.

It was but hours until her induction ceremony, and after that, wouldn't she be left to the same fate as her mother had suffered with Elithis? Would she be expected to give herself to a suitor, even though she was full with the growing life of Jesse's within? And what if Jesse did come? Would they let him take her, now?

Panic started gripping her, and she thought of the man in London who had tried to take her unwillingly and might have, had Jesse not come to her rescue. The thought sobered her, and she fought the urge to picture Serat forcing himself upon her. In a single moment, she had gone from a potential desire for him to a subtle fear of the man. Now, though it was invisible to her eyes, she could sense a cell around this place; a cage that she had willingly entered into without a plan of escape.

Serat must be leading the Oxychana now that Elithis was presumed dead, she thought. He must have gained every right and power, since Elithis' disappearance years ago. The thought had Evelyn looking at her mother and sensing that she too, was under this man's watchful eye. It gave her chills to think about crossing words with him and she forced a thin smile to her face while her backbone grew into a frozen length of rope. She dared not glance at the shoes again to confirm what she had seen, lest Serat lose confidence of his control, but the horrifying truth was apparent as she now saw his gaze fixed unbelievably upon the smiling moon hanging from her wrist.

XXI

The Cellars

Many times had Serat spent countless hours walking the lengths of the Oxychana leaf totem lines, flipping the leaves one by one and unlocking the secrets of their ancient past. This could only be done during daybreak, for candles and torches were far too dangerous to risk in the steamy underground chambers of the cellars.

Light would spill into the skylights on the eastern-most side of the lengthy subterranean dugout and the canopy high above was split in just the right manner to allow for this. The leaves themselves were preserved through a sauna process, maintained by the locals, who would rotate shifts daily. Rocks were super-heated over the flames of their nightly fires and were moved by thick steel tongs one by one to the four troughs of shallow water that sat parallel along the walls of the corridor. Before trading had begun, the water was also transported daily from the creek. Now, there was a valve that the daily worker would open briefly during their duties.

It was down here, in the place Serat stood again, that he had learned of the Heart of the Earth Mother. It was only by a union of the three that she would speak again. It would be the Sun, the Earth, and the Moon. Mohami had charged Serat with the deciphering of the totem lines, but he had not dared tell her of the repercussions of the triune.

The leaves told of a relic, but Serat thought it must be fable. If the three were to come together, the Earth would swallow up indifference and her Waters would gather together in one place. In one giant voice would her Winds cry out with torrents of twisting cyclones, and would unity only come through cleansing of the lands and the re-birth of the child of the Sun.

In his studies, Serat had long thought that that the union of three were merely an abstract representation of the time when the Earth and Moon would finally surrender to the many years of gravitational onslaught of the Sun and be swallowed up, giving rise to a new beginning.

As of late, he had found very descriptive figures within the leaves, claiming that the Heart of the Earth Mother lay dormant far beneath the Dolmen, in the recesses of her once magnificent Temple which now sat buried as if it were a tomb. And if not for this one leaf in particular, that bore two symbols, he may not have recognized the relic when it came.

He was risking the destruction of their very legacy with torch-fire that he now held close in the dark of the dugout. He was hungry to verify the one charred marking that meant union, and above it another that meant to raise.

This one leaf of the book-like collection, which ran along the line inside the corridor, sat between two others whose hieroglyphic meanings were obvious to anyone with eyes. Just as he had thought … on the proceeding side, a blazing sun upon the Earth, and falling aft, a smiling moon around Pangea.

Serat believed he had seen the Sun, and that it was now all but delivered to his hands, and the moon would be his upon the morning … inherited with his lovely bride to be. He sneered with wide, white teeth; a Cheshire's grin in the flickering dark.

There was Mohami now. Calling out for his assistance.

Serat extinguished the torch and rose from the cellars, proud in his cunning knowledge and intent on seizing the glory that was being so easily granted him. But he would soon find out that it would not be such a simple thing to take.

XXII

The Dolmen

Jesse's memory had failed him.

Waking up under the shifting shadows of the overhead Amazon forest was overly-stimulating for his mostly identical mental state, which shifted with each thought as he tried to catch it. The sweat suit that he wore reassured him as he recognized it as expensive, and this brought back to mind his trust fund and his father's death, but the out-of-place sandals on his feet brought him an uneasy and uncertain feeling. The sandals were dirty and worn.

Frustrated with himself. Jesse pushed himself up with one hand and searched his person for his cigarettes.

Whispering curses, he patted his chest, ass, and thighs twice over before finding his smokes where they usually hid.

He had always wanted his life to be a journey, and now he had it. Though he felt that journey had consisted of nothing more than hard liquor and drugs of a kind he could not recall, as of late.

A glimmer of blue shone behind flame as Jesse lit a cigarette. He let his body lean against a mound of rock that lay nearby to a bench that sat off of the route. Apparently, he had awakened in an alcove where a tourist may rest along the path.

Jesse slapped the dust from the front of his pants and blew smoke nonchalantly from his bottom lip while he peered up along the trail. While trying to gather his thoughts and get a grip on his bearings, the plaque before the chained-off cavern across the way caught his eye. A brass-studded silver plate that read:

Who but I can let known the secrets of the unhewn dolmen?
Who but I can make known the ages of the moon?
Who but I can find the secret resting place of the sun?
-Douglas Monroe

"*Who but I* would wake up in the middle of nowhere with a shabby pair of sandals on and an $1800 Dolce & Gabbana sweat suit?" he mumbled under his breath. Then, looking down at his own toes, atop the oddly out-of-place sandals, he remembered and thought to himself, 'Bad memories need good markers.'

A vague feeling drove his hanging hand to the small of his back where something was tucked. Grabbing a handful of stringy cloth he pulled it free. A key. The obviousness of his direction was refreshingly apparent.

Somehow he had managed to keep his wits about him, though whatever he had been drinking or smoking had really thrown him for a loop. Looking past the key now at the dirt and sandaled feet that strode toward the chained-off gate, Jesse could recall giving the man his Pumas ... and his word. The Oxychana man back at the village had risked his reputation for Jesse to peek within this ancient dwelling, and he had fallen asleep only feet from it.

The heaviness of the ancient padlock drew the key, now in Jesse's hand, to it with such gravity that he would dismiss his morning breath and headache. Absentmindedly, he'd accept the cigarette as a more than worthy substitute for toothpaste (of which he had none, anyway).

Working the key in the rusted metal clunker of a lock, he could spy the Dolmen beyond. It was a smooth trilithon of seven feet in height, stacked with stones to round it out like a tumulus. Its outermost circumference met the Earth in a sandy ring of foundation. Surrounding the ring was lush jungle growth, which contrasted sharply with the groomed appearance of the rounded structure. Golden light bathed the stone of the Dolmen and shadows danced across its surface in unison with the wind-blown shifting canopy.

As the lock came free, the chain's weight pulled the length of itself through the fence with noisy 'changs' and 'bangles'. Its descent to the forest floor ended in a dry thud. The lock—a heavy ancient treasure itself—would be among the pile of chain when he returned.

The fence had been only pushed open just enough to squeeze through sideways, tightly. The hinges were solidly rusted, and had not seen movement in years. The constant dampness of the rainy jungle air had played a role in this, no doubt.

Behind the gating, he now covered the few paces along the soft velvet carpeting of the jungle floor to the sandy reaches of the stone figure's base. Only a few huge elephant ears, leaves with shiny plastic-like coating, had prevented total viewing of the thing from directly out in front of it. But now they folded away like ancient feather fans that once had cooled Egyptian kings by the hands of their servants.

As he approached the foreboding, rounded megalith, a cooling sensation rose in his chest, as though a chill breeze permeated his outfit. Rounding the perimeter of the Dolmen revealed no entrance to the interior.

His fingertips reached out and gently felt of smooth stone while Jesse's other hand searched the surface with gentle pressure as if trying to push into the rock itself, hoping for perhaps a latch or pressure plate. Shuffling his feet sideways, he had continued feeling his way around the entire structure, when the sensation at his chest grew vividly cold, as if a block of ice was resting beneath his sweater.

With one hand, Jesse grasped the cord that held the amulet fastened around his neck and pulled it from within his suit. The amulet of sun was ablaze with a blue light so intense and cold it sent him twisting in the sand to free it from his body. Jostled, he yanked the cord hard, stumbling back against the face of the stone Dolmen, yet the solid face was no longer there. Instead, he felt his back strike the surface of a thin sheet of silky fabric that wavered beneath him, and the gut-wrenching feeling of sitting on a chair that had been removed consumed him. The total feel was like falling into a pillow case, and for a moment, he thought he may avoid a brutal landing.

To his disappointment, the sheet-like safety of the silk was stripped away and he could see the entrance in which he had fallen return to black above. Only for a split second the piercing ultraviolet light of the amulet lit the chamber within before he hit solid stone below.

XXIII

The Pursuit

Sweat was beaded on Evelyn's brow as she fled. The Quid which Serat had given her hadn't taken effect like he had wished. She had kept it rolled on her tongue until he had gone down to the cellars to verify what he had seen dangling on her wrist. Now the charm was gripped tight in her palm as she raced up the trail.

Three miles, she estimated, it would take to make it back into the Njaran slum, where she prayed that Greg had come back in search of her. If she could make it that far, she thought she might at least convince some of the folk to help her back to Owerre. The map and the small bag with her passport she had tucked under her arm, amongst the bundle of clothes which had sat beside her as Serat had gone about the task of coloring her as his bride.

Thunder struck above and the slightest sound of rain had begun to pitter the canopy and slowly maze its way through the loft of the forest ceiling, as if the weather itself were empathetic with her own fear. Looming darkness above and the night that had begun to overcome the sunlight—as her soul cried out silently for assistance—furthered this feeling in her.

She got a well-enough head-start when escaping from the hut, while her mother gathered up the herbs from the table into a leather pouch. Out the door and down the steps she fled, between the dual columns of tiki torches, which flickered in anticipation of the fading light. Evelyn had pictured steam billowing from the cauldron atop the needed fire at its summit as her mother screamed from behind her to stop.

"Do not defy us again, Evelyn! Come back!"

But she hadn't gone back! Nor did she ever intend to! Spitting that roll of Quid into the dirt as she breached her mother's hut had been the final time she ever would partake of the Oxychana poison.

Now her pace had slowed a bit, and she fought with the bundle of clothing, hoping to find the neck of her slip, but as she did, a dull horn-blast sliced through the air like a battle drum voicing her defiance to the world. She quickened her steps again, envisioning Serat donning the massive horn and setting his servants after her.

'If I can only make it to the site,' she thought, with a desperate hope. But that hope only prevailed another quarter-mile, when she heard something which would stop her dead in her tracks. Another dull horn-blast, rising up and bouncing back off the canopy to her ears. Yet this blast did not come from behind her in the village, it came from ahead, and it was close! Another blast, this time from behind, and then its equal again resounding out ahead in confirmation!

There was a stone bench here. Evelyn, now frantic with fear, crumpled down atop it and lay her bundle at her side, and with a thick, slow sigh she dropped her head and prayed.

When she was younger, she might have fled into the wild jungle and escaped, but she was grown now, and tired … tired of running … tired of lies … tired of fear. Above all, she was tired of *fear*. A desire in her had her insides burning to fight, growing angry that she been so blind and weak. The thought was accompanied by a feeling of warmth in her chest, a feeling of comfort, and as it began to set in she lifted her eyes to stand.

There had been no horns for minutes, and when Evelyn began to rise from the stone bench, her feet now melting into dimpled mud, she heard them closing in on her ahead. The falling rain made it hard to see deep enough down the trail to make them out, but there was another thing she saw. The mysterious stone Dolmen with the wavering entrance like an illusion—which she still magically could make out—stood only paces from her behind the gate.

'Maybe it is possible ... if I could only enter,' she thought.

The gate was just as it had been before, but now behind it lay a thick coil of rusted chain; among the pile, was the ancient open lock.

XXIV

The Light

Jesse had fallen hard onto solid stone. He remembered the fading light of the outside as he fell, and the azure glow that lit the air before he hit, while he lay semi-conscious within the darkness of his mind. It was for this reason, when the brightest light began to shine upon him as he winced and cracked his eyes into two thin slits, that he thought he was journeying into the afterlife. He squeezed his eyelids tight again. When they began to reopen, the light was a bit less harsh but still it sat motionless, suspended in a solid ball of rays, emitting from a central point above him. He could hear the sound of a voice, a beautiful voice, but a voice which was full of desperation. But he would not see the owner of this voice, not until he had first seen, and remembered, the talisman.

The sun, which was still ablaze with splendid blue light, lay only a pace away from where his head now lay, and he could feel the coolness of the energy coming back to him.

***

The entrance had been concealed. Evelyn had seen through its disguise, even before approaching it. It was only after grasping the fine material, which was silk-like in nature and feel, that she thought of what the Njaran woman had said. She had told her that rumor had it among children that the Great King Arthur, and that the Cloak of Paeden had housed special powers to hide his remains from the naked eye. She had seen, by no magical means at all, that the fabric had been pulled away at the edge, though she would have seen a flitting image by the power of the charm around her wrist, if it had not been so obvious. The cloak had been already disturbed, and she slowly pulled it back, as the moon hanging from her wrist, began to come alive with fire.

The heat from the smiling moon grew swift and fierce, a burning ember of its own power. She had pulled the trinket from her wrist and now held it in her left hand suspended out away from herself, dangling from the silver circlets, which had once kept it secure to her arm. It was like a lantern.

She could immediately make out a steep set of stone steps that wound their way down to the floor a body length below. But the light, by which she saw, did not come from only the object now outstretched in her hand, but rather from a brilliant point only feet below her, out in the middle of the room.

She had pulled the cloak back across the entry after she stepped in, but it was nothing short of absentmindedness, for below her, beyond the floating star of shimmering light, she could see her Love.

"Jesse?!" Evelyn's voice echoed down the well within the Dolmen and among stony walls.

Jesse was shifting, moving slowly now, shielding his eyes from the piercing brightness of the light that approached from above. From his point of view, the orb of white moved effortlessly, as does a skater on ice, first to the left it glided, and then grew bigger. Accompanied by the sound of approaching footsteps, the orb expanded, illuminating the interior of the cavern and bathing Jesse, himself, in a solid shell of pure light. But Jesse was not alone in this shell of light. There was now another, and was Jesse himself … still Jesse? He didn't know.

Evelyn's charm had been emitting an infrared light since she had entered here, and as she drew closer to Jesse she could see that his amulet had taken on its own glow, as well. It radiated with a brilliant ultraviolet, and it seemed that where the two waves of light met between them, the colors canceled one another out and formed a white orb of brilliance at its center. The whiteness grew, and the blue and red faded, as the two sources of these lights came close to one another.

The interior of the crypt-like place was now illuminated all around them, and Evelyn was taking Jesse up to her in an attempt to revel in those eyes she knew so well, those deeply penetrating eyes, which she had longed for endlessly.

Evelyn held Jesse's face between her hands as she knelt beside the spot where she had let the hot moon fall from her grasp and land beside the icy sun. It was Jesse's face, at last! She kissed him.

As her lips pursed slowly and she gently pulled away to look into his eyes, she was stricken with the sickly look that resided in them. There was no piercing gaze there; no depth emanated from his soul. There was only confusion and question in the mirrors looking back at her from within him. Her heart sank, and momentarily she pondered slouching here with him, in total ignorance of her impending fate.

The thought was stolen from her as the muffled familiar sound of the war horn rang out from above and beyond the entrance of the tomb. All hope that the Cloak of Paeden, if such was the mystical silken fabric that shielded the entrance from the eyes, washed away as she remembered leaving her bundled things resting on the bench across the path.

Surely they had seen the bundle and the broken lock, and they would undoubtedly begin searching for the entrance themselves, which was guarded by nothing more than an illusion. It wasn't comfort enough to stay here, she *must* move him, or else they would be upon her!

"Get up, Jesse!" she screamed, wrenching him strongly to his feet. "Get up! They're coming!"

She could see the bewilderment in his gaze now, but had no time to explain before they started moving. With one hand she reached down and seized the cord that held the sun, firmly forcing it as a bundle into his hand.

With the movement of the artifact, the sphere of light encompassing them pulsed as it swayed in his grip, pulling in on itself and restricting as if the distance between the two pieces were married to thc movement of the sphere itself.

"Hold this!" she insisted.

Then, leaning down and lifting her own amulet before her, "For light," she said, before tugging him toward the hollow that led down deep into the Earth.

The illumination from the two closely outstretched relics shone out in a distant radiance, which covered many yards ahead, revealing walls of ancient, untouched stone lining the throat of this subterranean tunnel.

The walls were scarred with lines of quartz crystal, which had been delicately scored into the surface rock, revealing the layer of the polished diamond-like element beneath.

At first glance, the twisting lines of reflecting quartz seemed randomly scored in eloquent curves, as if for nothing more than artistry. But, as the mouth of the tunnel swallowed them up, it was apparent that the chamber had indeed been purposely and intelligently carved into the likes of a cloudy thunderhead. For now, the sparkling lines shot down the walls in parallel strikes, resembling lightning from a looming overhead cloud.

"Wait!" The man pleaded with her.

Evelyn didn't resist his pressure too fiercely, in fear of scaring him into believing she was his enemy. The man's hand she held was Jesse's, but she knew the man inside was not.

"Not now," Gently now she spoke, sensing the questions in his eyes. "We haven't time. I'll explain along the way, but we gotta go, maybe the tunnel comes out at another point."

Evelyn cast her gaze up into the darkness, beyond the recess of the light from whence they had come. She heard the shuffling of sand and feet around the base of the Dolmen.

"Hear that? If they breach the shell, they'll be on us. Let's make some distance. Come on!"

Her hand was warm in his, and her face was reassuring. He let her lead him down through the stone catacombs, glancing over his shoulder once in a while, well aware that he could see nothing but pitch beyond the confines of the lighted bubble.

On and on they pressed, and he busied his eyes by fixing on the rivers of chiseled crystal lightning which snaked their way along the walls as Evelyn spoke.

She had begun by telling him her greatest fear, that Serat had done him harm, that she had spied his shoes on the man's feet and feared the worst … that the tribe was going to make her wed and bare her child as a Seeker.

It was during her recollection of their time together in London when they came upon a change in the quartz design. The bolts of lightning now crawled up huge marble columns on each side of the corridor. The reflective surface of the beautifully veined marble bore elaborate reproductions of the charms they each held. On the right, an image of the moon … on the left, the sun.

The light pulsed around them, and they each lifted their godly gifts up to see the detail in the designs, and the remarkable resemblance. The orb, which had surrounded them in a single mass, now parted down the center and moved like shadow from a setting sun. Slowly and methodically the white light regained its contrasting hues of red and blue, and the marble soaked up this color as if pooling it into the stone itself.

Momentarily they were plunged into the darkness among the center of the tunnel. The only light now emanated from the low frequency of the huge slabs, which had taken in the energy of the amulets. Then, as if flicking a switch on a fluorescent, each engraving flickered to life, like the neon lights of a low-end bar and grill.

The veins of color that ran deep in the marble filtered the same light into the channel of quartz beyond, this time following a perfectly straight path along the center of each wall, like the slowly sizzling fuse of a firecracker.

Now, in the dimly lit hollow of the tunnel, Evelyn approached her Jesse. Taking his half of the relic, she locked it tight to hers, hoping to spark recognition in him as she revealed to him the story of the *gift*, and the true nature of the growing life within her.

A look of growing concern and contemplation was pasted across the canvas of Jesse's face, and in desperation she embraced him, her lips a fraction from his ear.

"Yours, the sun that's filled with shining light that blazes far and wide. Mine, the moon, which reflects the sunlight back, but has no light inside. Together we can shine anew, a living breathing light. In union once again in life, that Mother Earth provides."

Pressing her lips to his, she kissed him—and this time—oh, how she kissed him!

A dizzy spell of recognition flushing through him, he clasped her in his arms.

"Evelyn. My Evelyn," he whispered.

Momentary panic sent shudders down his spine, but as quickly as he remembered, he repressed the old thoughts of his father.

"I knew you would come, my love. I couldn't believe that you would stay away from me, when my heart longed for you so deeply!" she exclaimed.

"Not in three lifetimes," Jesse said, now aware of the neon-lighted quartz stretching out into the dark before them.

"Serat said," then focusing on the relic, "this is foretold to reunite the segregation of mankind. The truth is written here in the stone of these columns. Whatever lies in wait down there, is something they were willing to take against our will to obtain. It is rightly ours, my love."

An echo came from behind in the darkened abyss, which turned their blood to ice.

"Evelyn!!" The voice cried out in desperation, as the dim flicker of torchlight spotted the distant void.

“Let’s go!” Jesse said through hurried breaths, and they began chasing the line of light which stretched steadily into the beyond.

XXV

The Chamber

The Cloak of Paeden … Serat had always thought it a myth. But now he saw how the entrance to the Dolmen had eluded his people for all this time. There was a simple cape of magical properties that the builder here must have used to hide this important place. But did this tomb really house the remains of the ancient King that the researchers had spoken so avidly about? He was rather sure it did not. Either way, he would find out if the oracle of the ancient leaf houses were true.

When Serat's servants had found the bundle of Evelyn's on the bench adjacent to the dome, he knew she would be within. Now she would be with Jesse for sure, and that meant that they possessed the relic in its entirety. He asked himself why he hadn't forced the thing from her when he had the chance. No worries though, as long as he could catch them before they activated the ancient device, he would be safe.

"They know not what they do," he muttered lowly as he moved, hidden under the protective cloak of invisibility, gaining slowly on them each minute, the new shoes he wore profoundly increasing his speed.

***

Along the wall to Evelyn's right, the deep infrared line of light began tracing at first, perfect circles and spirals as they rushed along. Five minutes later, the designs began taking on more prominent figures resembling simple seashells, then intricate conchs. Another three minutes into the depths and the light traced its way through the fine lines of clams, perfect shrimp and simple arthropods like crab and lobsters.

The sight was spellbinding along Jesse's left as well for ultraviolet spirals of blue became seedlings and seedlings became sprouts. They resisted the urge to slow their pace and take in the miraculous sight of the perfect images, though the pull was strong to do so. As the crystal carvings became more intricate in nature, also did the illusion that each took a breath of life as they illuminated.

The red flame of torchlight behind them had gone, and the stretch of tunnel leading back up was lit with enough colored light to see a good distance, and there was no one. Of course, if Serat had moved beyond the darkness he would not need a torch to light his way.

Once he made it to the columns of red and blue he would see well enough. But as far as a sign of him, they had none.

Now the picture perfect designs of light were more frequently appearing. They were gaining on the tip of the advancing flow of color through the quartz lines. Once they caught up with it, they would have no choice but to slow their pace, for it would be far too dark to outrun it.

They were deep now within the Earth, approaching the heart of the Earth Mother herself. A cavern of this magnitude could only be one of the single greatest endeavors of races past. The massive slabs of stone that lined the interior of the cave fit together so precisely that even a single sheet of paper would not fit between them. This construction was doubly astounding, for not a bit of mortar, visible to the naked eye, held these stones in place. Each one must have been so precisely machined that they fit together firmly, like pieces of an elaborate puzzle. The floor was constructed in a similar fashion, yet thousands, perhaps millions, of oddly shaped granite blocks were seamlessly placed, only the keenest sight could ever see the joints.

The neon red now snaked its way through images of fish, salamander, turtle, snake, lizard and bird. At the same time, the blue became involved in tracing the fine lines of a flower, fly-trap, bee, caterpillar, rodent, bat, jungle-cat, lemur, and monkey.

They overcame the pace of the racing light as it took on the meticulous task of igniting huge collages of men. On the left, they portrayed the immense process of domesticating animals, and on the right, the miracle of conception and childbirth. It was only when the horizontal lines of advancing colors finally assumed a mirror image of one another that the walls took on a new feature.

Unbelievable numbers of men lit up brightly in line, all united in a single effort, pictured climbing step after step up blocks hewn from the purest gold. The wall beyond the first touch of treasured twenty-four karat, was made of nothing but the most precious metal.

Parallel to one another, the men worked to push huge blocks of the gold up the steep grade of a massive pyramid. Above them opened into a giant cavern of vaulted ceilings and the walls widened drastically before turning back on themselves.

Stretching up before them loomed a solid wall of gold where the two sides of the endless corridor finally came to meet. A great pyramid of epic proportion, when compared to the men that walked upon it, stretched up the length of the wall. It was capped with a perfect triangle depicting the All Seeing Eye, which now began to shine in a pure white light as the two beams of contrasting neon met behind it.

The two stood in awe as the bright white light began to peek through an invisible seam in the gold. A doorway was emerging directly in the center of the huge wonder right at floor level. Brighter the light grew by each second until the door seemed suspended in the golden wall, separated by an inch of light surrounding the massive shape, yet looking weightless and unaffected by gravity.

Jesse approached the golden door, his shifting reflection looking back at him through hazy recognition as he reached out to push open the tremendous entranceway. Evelyn's hand fell lightly on his shoulder as the titanic gateway swung slowly back, her mouth languidly falling open at the spectacle.

The gigantic portal opened on a perfectly equilateral room, not nearly as immense as the antechamber but exceedingly majestic. The floors were a polished mirror surface, and as the glow receded up into the cavity above the door, Jesse's eyes followed it to the smudged silver ceiling emerging overhead while he entered. Evelyn cautiously trailed behind letting her hand fall sluggishly to her side as she surveyed the walls around her.

To the right was a towering wave of gold and jewels etched into the stone; poised to crash devastatingly onto a man clad in silver armor bracing against a silver shield to protect himself from the onslaught of riches. The wall to the left depicted a man clad in golden robes bearing a flaming sword, seemingly commanding an immense pile of silver into a looming force field.

A sound from behind sent Evelyn spinning quickly around, but just then the crack of thunder rolled above and the white light from above the door shot fiercely up into the above canopy of smoky gray, spidering the ceiling with strikes of lightning. The effect was a perfect representation of a thunderhead rolling with ball lightning before a storm. It wasn't until the cloud rolled with thunder and ignited the room for a final time, that they saw the back wall light up and reveal what waited there.

The uppermost branches of the tree, that occupied the surface of the back bulkhead, was inlaid with millions of green emeralds, and the stone that provided for its trunk was carved directly from the cavern's petrified rock, which had experienced eons of water erosion, giving it a deeply weathered brownish texture. To the left the sun, to the right the moon—even now they began to radiate with the pure whiteness of energy.

Sitting at the base of the massive emerald oak were the statues of a naked man and woman. They were positioned in such a way that their bodies seemed to meld together at the hip, where each had their inside knee bent skyward from a cross-legged posture. They had an arm around one another's shoulder and their other hands met out in front of them as if in offering. The whites of their eyes had been cast from the same creamy quartz crystal that had been carrying the light through the corridors. Their blank stares were almost hypnotizing atop the mirrored floor that reflected the simulated sky above, which now sat in still illumination from the rivers of light within the foreboding clouds.

As if sensing the thoughts of the couple, the room began to whir with the sound of static electricity, much as a storm cloud before an imminent crash of lightning. Then, in a single instant a brilliant flash came from above and a silver streak of pure light shot down the back wall and through the very center of the great emerald oak to the floor.

A kaleidoscope of every image that had riddled the walls in their descent, from the first spirals to the last birds and creatures, shone out from the intricate leaves of the jeweled tree of life. The eyes of the embracing statues came full on blazing white, and their outstretched hands now danced with a fluctuating crown of rotating color in their palms. Evelyn gasped as the amulet in her hand swam with a rainbow of shiny accuracy mirror-imaging the flowing color in the stone couple's grasp.

As a holographic image of Earth shimmered into being and rotated in the center of the wavering crown a voice boomed within the chamber, as if God himself commanded them.

"Eve. The relic, now!"

But it wasn't the voice of a deity.

It was too late when Jesse saw its origin in the surface of the floor behind where Evelyn stood, reflecting an image that he knew all too well … his old Pumas.

XXVI

The End of the Beginning

With a single motion of haste, Serat pitched the cloak away from around his shoulders, his form rolling into view as the material was swept away. The air shimmered as the garment twisted in the chamber to the floor and Serat seized Evelyn with one strong arm around the neck and shoulder. Evelyn gasped, dropping the cascading color-rung amulet and clenching her fingers into the forearm of her assailant. Jesse lurched toward her in a valiant effort, but as he grasped the arm that was around her neck Serat had unsheathed his massive kukri blade with its curved and hardened steel. Anger and desperation flowed in Serat's blood; now the decision to take this man's life was final in his mind. The sharpened steel in his hand was his glory … the fact that he had let this man live, his only regret.

Serat's raised the ferocious knife up, poised to finish this man once and for all. Bringing it down hard to Jesse's chest and piercing his heart would rid this world of him …

… but the blade stopped short.

Jesse's left hand gripped the hilt and Serat's fist in one giant grab. Forcing against the dark man's immense strength, Jesse only a match for him because he was driven by pure adrenaline, kept him waveringly at bay. When the pressure became too much, he had to release the arm that captured Evelyn to him tight and add his right hand to the chore.

Taking a knee on the mirrored floor, succumbing to the great brute's sheer force, Jesse clenched his teeth, willing his arms to not fail him. He was moments from exhaustion when Serat pulled back the knife and cried out in pain, throwing Evelyn to the smooth surface, sending her sliding into the wall as thunder struck again.

Once more, the silver bolt of lightning ignited through the majestic oak and increased the blaze of the stone beings' eyes yet further.

Evelyn slumped, wiping a small dot of blood from her mouth where she had bitten hard into the cusp of his elbow. She struggled to catch her breath and watched as Serat leaned to grab up their amulet, which radiated a rainbow of movement.

"You know nothing of such power," Serat said, as his fingers brushed the wavering object.

Jesse had pressed himself to his feet and with an all-out war cry, he charged.

With low grunts and a crack, Jesse's shoulder drove ferociously into Serat's ribs, sending him reeling backwards. The short sword clattered to the floor, and Jesse toppled over him, his shoulder sore and bruised.

Serat had easily broken a rib, but wasted no time in rolling sideways and mounting Jesse, pinning his head by forcing his elbow into his throat under his weight. Jesse wheezed and groped at the man's arms and body to no avail; he would black out in seconds.

Serat's right elbow came down hard to Jesse's face with a thud, softened only by his hands flailing in defense. A second blow wouldn't have been so forgiving had Serat not been wrenched from behind by Evelyn, in the same manner he had come upon her. He grabbed at her overhead, wincing at the shooting pain through his ribcage, and his elbow came away from Jesse's throat, though he was still attempting to keep a forceful grip on his face, fingers digging in to the cheeks.

A large bundled grip of Evelyn's fine hair was clenched in Serat's strong fist. Evelyn tripped, falling backward to the floor as he drove rearward with his powerful legs. Still, she managed to hold tight to his throat through the fall, but his hand had come to rest inches from his downed weapon.

Jesse still lay nearby, between the corner and the backside of the massive golden door, the interior side coated with the same perfect pewter as the rest of the chamber. He was pushing himself up on an elbow gasping for air to reopen his windpipe, which had been nearly crushed. Evelyn watched in horror as Serat seized the cord-bound handle of the deadly kukri once more, and she momentarily thought of rushing away to safety.

It was in that split second that Serat pried her away from him by the hair and jerked her scalp hard, flinging her to the corner, where Jesse still lay recovering. Both he and Evelyn were crumpled together now in the corner. Jesse pulled her close to him, comforting her but still showed no sign of cowardice as Serat took his full height and towered over them.

"You shouldn't be here. You are not of Oxychana blood! Only Oxychana are permitted to close the great rifts and rid the world of segregation. And you, Evelyn, I would have had *you* as my ka-tet, you blaspheme by deception and deceit!"

Serat breathed a great breath, filling his painful lungs and hiding his agony behind clenched teeth.

"You both will meet your Gods this day, and I will bring pride to the tribe as it is written. No man of the New World could ever know how to seed a new land, and no harlot could raise his young."

Serat spoke from meager satisfaction at his own voice and smiled wryly at his knowledge of the leaf totem. But as he went on, and readied himself to slay the couple where they sat, Jesse's mind swam into the past and dug into once painful memories of his father's journals. He silently surveyed Evelyn's face, oblivious to any of Serat's words which had come after that one potent phrase: '**You are not Oxychana.**'

Jesse sensed the fierceness in Serat's voice and watched his grip tighten on the halberd as he spoke. His intentions were true, but misguided, and if they were not misguided, they would instead be brandished by selfishness, the same selfishness that had motivated the tribesman to send him away from Evelyn, and the same selfishness that demanded his shoes. Knowing the man was not apt to respond to reason, the looming blade positioning itself to come down upon them, drew Jesse into action.

Raising a hand in defense and composing himself low to the ground before Evelyn, he lashed out with words of his own.

"I may not be Oxychana! But the same blood flows in my veins!"

At this, Serat paused, and for the first time Evelyn spied something *similar to Jesse* in Serat's quizzical expression. An expression that was lost immediately to anger.

"Liar! That is not possible!"

"Years ago, my father, James Bankole, came to this tribe following the map that *you* confiscated from my possession. It was here that he met my mother, the woman whose photograph you bear this very instant! The woman …" His words faded as he saw the color in Evelyn's cheeks run dry at the statement. " … who also bore Evelyn."

The look on Evelyn's face told Serat that she saw truth in this, that she knew the name James Bankole, and Serat himself knew that name, *James,* as well. Many times had he listened to the story of Mohami's betrayal that gave her Evelyn, and now he was face-to- face with the same betrayal under his *own* command. His rage grew within him like water fills a sponge, and the blasphemy of the whole situation sent him into a blind fury like never before.

In his madness he screamed, “You know not what you do!”

With this, Jesse threw himself protectively over Evelyn, wrapping her in a bodily embrace, just as a clap of lightning again sent a resonating boom through the doorway and out into the tunnel.

Now the eyes grew intensely whiter and perfect cones of light erupted from their sockets, bathing the giant entrance in a white, translucent blanket.

“Serat!” a voice came crying out authoritatively from beside the frozen statues of stone.

Serat turned to it, completely off guard, to see a man who he was no more familiar with than he was with Jesse.

It was Greg—the Djinn.

***

A human Greg would have been reluctant to leave her in this place. Perhaps there was humanity left in him after all.

He knew the moment she set off along that trail with those ladies from the slum that he would never forgive himself were something to befall her. He had been silent for most of the ride back to Owerre, which was uneventful besides when they had been passed by in a narrow gully by another shabby vehicle. In the backseat was a man, he was sure was Jesse, but a brief wave only brought a confused stare from the gentleman. So when he reached the city he made sure to properly pay his guide for a return trip in the morning.

Greg had entertained himself by revisiting the local library and determining how much of the truth researchers had uncovered while studying the Dolmen and Arthurian lore, which the area seemed to be noted for. Within the local writings, available to the public near the card catalogs, he found an article by the archeologist who had resided among the Njarans in the late seventies.

Found around the Njaran village, and near where was fabled to be a West African entrance to underground cities of Ancient Atlantean natives—who were supposed to have washed ashore after the cataclysm during the age of Pangea—were remnants of stone which originated thousands of miles away. The questions that stumped the journalists and historians were many. Among them were the few pieces of information that linked the tunnels to a subterranean system, stretching South-East into African territory populated by the richest deposits of Silver and Gold on Earth. This had heavily contrasted with the origin of the bluestone fragments found at the site, which came from the Northwest region in the country of Wales.

Thumbing through the Arthurian Legend he was reminded of his own distant past.

Merlyn, a druid of Anglesey, had mentored the young King, after his Catholic upbringing and before his reign. The boy was a notable figure in the Celtic world for his birth on Beltane, the Summer Solstice, making him a child of the Sun God Belinus.

Arthur had been put through a series of Pagan initiations to ensure that he would be fair to the Pagans and Christians alike, as the new religion sought to push Paganism from the area for good. The marriage of Arthur to a Catholic bride, Gwenyffar, was to ensure a stable base to his reign.

Their Celtic union, performed at the site of legendary Stonehenge, was symbolized by an amulet forged from the mountains of Snowdonia. Arthur's made from the bluestone, found only at the mountains base, and plated in gold. The queen's crafted from the rare red ruby of Mars, found only at the mountain's highest peak, and then plated with silver. Presented to them by Merlyn, the two were fabled to always wear their jewelry, much like wedding bands of the present.

How colorful the past of the Djinn's existence! How close they got to right! How a race so far removed from the origins of Father Time's creation could dredge up such memories for him sent him to bed feeling as ancient as the years of knowledge bestowed on him by the Crone. In the night, his heart had stirred.

When morning had come, he was a bit undecided to return so early. The last thing he wanted was to be sitting at that site, where he would undoubtedly be hassled for money or favors, at length. His escort had been busying himself with other customers in the city anyhow, so he waited 'til evening before calling on him.

There were people gathered at the plank leading into the jungle when they arrived and his guide had gotten quite worried by the sight, as if he had seen this behavior before.

It had taken no time for Greg to find out what was going on and push his way past the frail people of this small village and onto the trail. He may have been an outsider, but he was in no way an active threat to anyone. It was by chance that he happened upon the small messenger boy halfway up the trail and offered him a handful of francs for a bit of information.

***

Now, Greg stood in perfect posture, the teal of his suit dancing with the wavering crown of the colored circuit. In his hand he held the amulet by the bundled cord. It was suspended over the palms of the accepting hands of the solid figures, whose lighted round of rainbow now reached up high, in colored waves like a lover's lips enticing a kiss.

The golden portal, from whence they had entered, now reflected the white of the gazers' eyes and the outline of the door's original inset shimmered as it had upon opening. Serat was oblivious to it, and even dared the strange light that was spilling from the two works-of-arts' stares, as he crossed the distance in two great strides screaming in plea.

"No!"

Greg's intent was lost to him as the sturdy man charged, but was devoid for his own safety, knowing that the servants of Serat would be close behind him.

He had rushed into the entrance of the open Dolmen after the Njarans had told him of the breach and pursuit. Upwards of eight of Serat's followers stood, not far from the open site, with brandished torches, and had witnessed him enter in haste. They surely were inspired to follow shortly after, and if Greg had turned his head to peer back up the tunnel, he would have verified this fear by spotting the array of swaying torchlight approaching. But he would never have the time.

The blade of the kukri plunged deep into Greg's stomach as Serat grabbed his wrist, which grasped the bundle, knocking it loose. Blood ran from the tip and down the edge of the blade as it protruded from Greg's back. His head cocked back, the muscles of his neck tightening in an expression showing both pain and strength.

The amulet fell, as the shadows of light and dark moved within the chamber where lightning ran the length of the ceiling again and again. Barely avoiding contact with its begging twin, the cord caught the tip of one outstretched stony finger, and snagged to a subtle swinging motion below it.

Evelyn's hand covered her mouth in terror as she screamed, "Greg!"

Jesse pushed himself to his feet, and saw in the shifting lights of silver, Greg lock on his gaze with a telling stare. He watched as Greg powerfully grabbed the handle of the kukri, trapping Serat's hand to his body and smiling fiercely through gritted teeth at him.

He heard him mutter through the vice of his clenched jaw, "Let us test the extent of your gift, dear Crone."

Then Greg forced Serat toward the entrance of the chamber, only then seeing the crowd of servants gathering close outside.

Jesse had moved around the massive door from the corner where it had been invisibly hinged, and was going to join the struggle when he saw the number of tribesmen closing in to help their battling leader.

With a spray of blood upon the pelt over Serat's shoulder, Greg called out with all his remaining vocal strength, "Jesse! The door!"

As he watched his friend failing in his strength, and while Serat pulled the silver blade from his guts with obvious pain, Jesse backed a step in reverse and reached for the door, but Evelyn had already put it in motion.

Like a puck upon ice it slid, pivoting with ease. Serat, who lurched to stop it in its tracks, left Greg to fall down in a bloody pile at his feet, but was stopped short.

Greg held his foot, which was dressed in Jesse's attire, with all his might and smiled as the gargantuan golden plate fell back flush against the humbling pyramid.

***

From within, Evelyn turned her back to the silver inside of the door and slid down to the floor between the fading outline of the now-closed entrance. The light around the door diminished into matching contrast with the surrounding pewter wall forming a perfect invisible seal.

Jesse knelt beside her, breathing heavily and taking her hands in his own. The intense light of the lifelike statues began drawing back into themselves as she gradually met Jesse's eyes. The pendant still swung like a pendulum from the finger of the stone, and the dancing ring of color in its palm regained a calmer fluctuation once again.

"Is it true, my love? Was it your father that my mother met in the forest by this Dolmen so long ago?"

"I found his journals in the States. A picture of your mother rested within the same pages as a perfect map of your tribe's region, pinpointing Oxychana directly. Whether we are of the same blood I could not know for sure, but I feared the worst." Jesse told her.

"My mother told me on my night of arrival that she had met a man at this Dolmen, directly defying Oxychana rule, much as I had done myself."

She looked at him in timid exhaustion.

"Still, Love, there is no proof that a link exists between us for certain, save our feelings for one another," he offered.

Lightning flashed now in the chamber and the looming towers of gold and silver reflected the glare in a beauty of unsurpassed abundance. In the refracting light she gazed at him in a look that revealed a bit of hardened guilt, "My mother ... She told me his name … His name was James."

Dropping her head momentarily, she looked up again, bravely meeting his stare with teary eyes, "I'm full with child, my love. It is ours. Of this ... I have no doubt."

Jesse turned his gaze to the emerald tree behind him, contemplating the words of the holy man from New York, who had taken him but as an opportunity, and another blaze of lightning found its way through the leaves of the oak and down through its trunk.

As the holographic images from the tree of life danced again in the shadowy chamber, Jesse turned to her.

"There was a time, my dear Evelyn, in the beginning, that we all were of one blood, and came from one blood. Do not misjudge yourself as sinner when there was nothing in our actions or thoughts that defiled our beliefs. We both acted from only the purest place in our hearts. I, as my God did in creation."

She dared a small warm smile, "And I, as did the Earth Mother in her own."

Taking her by the hand to her feet he embraced her, kissing her lovingly and supporting the small of her back. His hands found their way around the front of her hips to the vague roundness of her lower abdomen where he sensed the warmth of life within, his eyes assuring his acceptance and emotion.

If the small army of Serat's were still trying to gain access again to the chamber, they were unobservant. If not for the workings of the extravagant effects of thundering light, the chamber's interior would have been as silent as a tomb.

It was only after their moment of confident reunion had passed that their heads would turn in unison, as the lighted eyes of the frozen stone people grew thick again with luminosity.

They stared in silence as the pools of light neared again the point the silver door had occupied in the wall minutes ago. Both knew that if the seal around the door grew light again, it could be pressed open from the other side, and Serat's company would easily be able to overpower the two of them alone.

The time had come to act.

XXVII

Egypt

On the surface, Abbott Bruner had been studying Egypt, especially the Great Pyramid and the Sphinx, for years uncounted. It was his duty, passed down generations from father to son, to maintain records of those who entered the structure. Every spec of the site had been logged in the volumes that impregnate the Plantation library back in the States.

The Egyptologist had his wife in from Southern Seoul, and she was attending his trademark amateur expedition, with which he often got too carried away. Each year, around the same time, he would take a group of Americans up close to the ancient sites and reiterate on the more interesting aspects of the culture. Anna, Abbott's wife, was among the handful of people as they approached the Giza site on camelback.

Abbott started with his dialogue, "The Great Pyramid, of course, is immensely heavy and could only be supported by a mountain of substantial stone. Indeed, a flat, solid, granite mountain happens to be located just beneath the sub-surface of the terrain, but people speculate as to whether the foundation is natural or part of the monumental wonder which drives even deeper below the surface."

Jarred, a senior student in paleontology at UGA, looked questionably at Abbott before asking him, "Have there not been expeditions in to the site, Abbott? Doesn't someone know for sure what lies beneath?"

The pyramid's majestic size was monumental in relation to the smaller surrounding adobe buildings of rectangular design, which suffered past erosion with elegant posterity.

Abott confounded himself on many occasions with the secrets he held so dear. He knew, for instance, that Giza was the only pyramid that had both ascending and descending passageways, as if someone were meant to climb up, rather than the traditional descent to a tomb. He also knew that no burial tomb was ever found in the great interior of the megalithic structure.

"Well, lad, archaeologists have been more than lucky that Egypt has allowed expeditions into any sites at all. It is a delicate subject. But sometimes, it is in the contemplation of such mysteries that we find other discoveries of the imagination."

Anna smiled to herself, noting her husband's tact as he continued.

"Does someone have an American dollar bill with them?" Abbott asked the group, bidding the camel to a halt among them.

The woman dressed in the beige safari walkabout, her hair twisted into a sandy blonde bun under a brimmed hat, pulled a crumpled bill from the pocket of her vest and handed it to him.

Untangling the note and smoothing it on the leather strapping of the camel, he lifted it to eye level before the pyramid, "You can see here the pyramid on the right of the note, and, see the uppermost piece how it is separated from the base. Note the inclusion of the All-Seeing-Eye of Ra on the capstone. Some say it symbolizes the fact that we can only see a small percentage of the actual megalith today. How the rest of such a giant could be buried so deep into solid Earth is another mystery itself."

The camels lumbered on toward the Great Pyramid, approaching the velvet roped-off entrance to the tourist line.

"It is built to face true North. The actual odds of this pyramid being placed where it is are less than one in three billion, for it falls directly on the very center of the Earth's landmass, at zero-degree latitude and zero-degree true longitude. The Greenwich Observatory in London was long thought to be the prime meridian, because that is where the Royal Observatory clock is kept in conjunction with true world time, known as Greenwich Mean Time. Seconds a year are added to keep its time in tune with universal expansion and contraction."

Abbott slid from atop his mount and motioned that the group tie their camels to the wooden post aside the crowded mini-market, where locals bartered miniature figurines and replicas of mummified remains. Helping Anna down, he smiled warmly at her, pulling her thin bonnet properly under her chin before kissing her.

"At the base of the Giant again, Anna. Will it ever get old?" he asked her.

Jason from Harvard finished tying his camel's bit to the wood and approached Abbott and his wife with a question, "These blocks were quarried from miles away?"

"Some say they were, among which are blocks weighing multiple tons. But what you see now was not the way this pyramid would have looked thousands of years ago. What was seen then was much more impressive."

"How so, Abbott?"

The others had gathered closely by as he explained, "At completion, the Great Pyramid was surfaced by white casing stones. Casing stones were blocks of highly polished white limestone, resembling quartz. These were carefully cut to an approximate slope and reflected the surrounding light. Visibly, all that remains is the underlying stepped core structure seen today."

Anna stared up at the massive capstone as she listened to the eager questions of the group.

"So, what is typically within these pyramids?"

Abbott found the question very general and decided to up the ante a bit. "Most are reported to be burial chambers for highly-powerful monarchs, but many were found to be looted of the treasures, that were buried with the dead, long before any documented excavation could be performed. The problem with exploring these twisting tunnels is that very little oxygen reaches down into the vast depths of the furthest chambers. Torches won't burn in the furthest reaches of the tombs, only electric lights of our modern time, provide ample vision to explore in those depths."

"But Abbott, if only electric light can burn within the confines of the deeper chambers, how did the ancient peoples manage to decorate these tombs?"

"An excellent question Andy, and a question that has baffled some scientists as well, even to this day! One theory suggests that the purpose of the many ventilation shafts was to provide such needed oxygen and light, but now many of these shafts have caved in, or are misaligned from their original positions leaving no real way to tell for sure."

"And another theory?"

Anna shot her husband a disapproving glance, but followed it with a smile when she saw she could not cool his passion for such conversation.

"Well, Andy, the World as you know is bountiful with very strange occurrences, such as when they discovered a perfectly machined cube of metal within a billion year old coal shaft, or the time paleontologists unearthed dinosaur bones with bullets embedded in them. The World of archeology has also its strange findings. Ancient batteries have been found in Egyptian tombs, made from the citric acids of indigenous fruits and copper. Some believe they used these batteries and copper wire to illuminate the inner chambers as they worked."

"Batteries? I thought the battery wasn't invented until the early eighteen-hundreds. Giza itself must be thousands and thousands of years old!" the sandy-haired woman exclaimed.

"Thousands?" Abbott Bruner chuckled softly. "Dating claims Giza and the surrounding structures, including the Sphinx, were estimated to be built right around twenty-five-hundred BC. Others claim it to be ten to fifteen thousand years old."

She looked at him nodding softly.

"I know! Quite impressive. If the whole battery thing throws you for a loop, you should know that there are Aztec caverns that far outdate this site, which house pictures of man seemingly wearing full space suits, and as you know, space exploration didn't begin until the nineteen-hundreds. It's all quite baffling."

Anna straightened her posture and pulled Abbott back a bit, "Now don't go sending their young minds off somewhere else, Honey. I think we all are here to learn a bit more about this culture in particular."

With a whimsical nod, Abbott pointed a finger out into the sandy distance, where the Sphinx stood majestically, "Ah yes, of course. Take the Sphinx, for example. Did you know they say the gaze of the eyes point directly to a binary star system called Sirius which, in many ancient writings, is told to be where the gods came from to Earth, that star in particular being the brightest in the sky? The pyramid, itself was fabled to represent the bottom half of an hourglass full of sand, representing the end of something and the beginning of another. Legend has it, that when universal alignment comes with the Dog Star Sirius and its neighboring black hole, this new beginning will take place."

Andy, suddenly very intrigued, stepped up and spoke, "And when is this alignment supposed to take place?"

Smiling and glancing around at them, Abbott put one arm around the shoulder of his wife, "Well, my boy. Why do you think I was so adamant about being here this afternoon?"

"It is today?" Andy exclaimed, in question.

Abbott Bruner laughed heartily at his reaction and reached a hand out to rest on his shoulder, "Lad, I would also tell you that many have speculated the Great Pyramid's location to be ample evidence that it was constructed as the original Tower of Babel. There are so many theories, my boy, that I believe we have nothing imminent to worry about."

The last he'd said may have been too much. Secretly, Bruner's family had been dreaming of seeing this temple open since time immemorial. He was here precisely for the same reason, and though colleagues found him foolish, he couldn't discount a chance to clear his family name.

Christi was still busying herself with her camel's bit, and was having a time fighting with it, as she tied it to the corral post. Something had it spooked. And as she called to the group for help, a plume of sand drifted down from the top of the Great Pyramid's capstone, as if the whole thing had shifted from above.

Now, people pointed up to the megastructure, as waterfalls of sand cascaded down the stepping sides of the monument toward its base. It was as if a vibration within had set this act in motion. The camels sensing it, neighed and tore free from their loose bindings, clumsily running out away from the pyramid into the desert.

As the beating feet of the fleeing camels faded, a deep sound like the grinding of a mortar and pestle, dominated the air, and the sand around Giza began moving as a single unit in a counter-clockwise motion. Slowly it churned around its base, as if an unseen giant stirred it like a huge pot of pea soup.

"My God," said Abbott, "it's opening!"

And as light emanated from now prominent slits in the capstone, he realized that it was not the sand moving at all. He gasped in utter astonishment, when the realization came clear that the turning object was the Great Pyramid itself!

From behind shifting sands at the base, he could spy a cavity dark as pitch. His eyes widened.

The Tower of Babel was not simply opening …

… it was rising!

XXVIII

The Opening

Evelyn stood across from Jesse watching the ring of mesmerizing pastels and shifting hues dance between them. There was no choice but to go on, and the fear that may have been associated with the act returned to the sense of wonder they had felt when they first shared this artifact back in London. What a perfect reflection of their love! And here they stood, Evelyn now reaching her right hand out and taking Jesse's beneath the awaiting torrent of color.

"I think, my Love, that I had found the man of the Sun a long time ago. I could have known it was you all along." She watched him take up the cord of the suspended amulet and raise it to the altar.

"And I, the one person I had always prayed to meet." He smiled at her and blessed her with his ever-present tact, "They say we men always end up marrying our mothers."

She laughed … and the fingers of light reached up once again in a beckoning gesture of desire, but this time slowly crawled upon the relic's surface as Jesse lowered it to its seat within the hologram, meeting Evelyn in a kiss over the open hands of the now silent statues.

The hologram wavered, as the amulet slowly stood upright to fit itself perfectly behind the flawless reproduction. The ceiling grew still for a moment, and the two pieces of the charm began to again emit a dull glow of their own colors. The moon again waxing with its infrared, and the sun which lay behind it an azure ultraviolet.

Now, the center of the pendant began radiating a florescent, olive glow across the depicted Super Continent. And the light, which riddled the ceiling randomly above, started to drain slowly from the entrance wall toward the emerald tree of life. As the lightning continued filtering its every photon down into the trunk of the great, standing stone timber, the fingers of the once still adamantine people came alive with motion.

Jesse and Evelyn backed away from the surreal, awakening couple in exact union of the draining light of the above. The fingers of each hand smoothly moved to embrace the levitating relic, twisting the pieces apart and separating them, leaving now the images' blurry aftermath of the once distinct hologram.

Each hand moved slowly away from one another, and the sitting figures now astonishingly were beginning to rise to their feet. They moved mechanically up before the tree, via a large, stone slab attached behind them, which had begun to lift as if the gathering light were acting like water lifting a cork as it fills a vessel.

In unison of this humbling movement, each figure clasped its own relic to its chest until the light from each had been hidden from sight. The stormy ceiling above momentarily went dark, as the last lines of lightning drained down through the glistening emeralds of leaves upon the oak.

Jesse was caught hypnotically by the growing gaze of the male rock figure, and so he failed to notice the small point of light which had begun growing in the opening lid of the chamber.

Evelyn's eyes were staring upward at the glowing shoestring circle above. Coming through as a golden ray, the light shaft fell directly upon her. There was a subtle shift, which unbalanced her momentarily, and she pictured herself standing on a slowly accelerating carousel. She turned to Jesse, her head now covered in the growing yellow light, but he was oblivious.

His blank stare was locked tight on the eyes of the statue, as if he could hear it speaking to him by inaudible means. Evelyn thought of stepping in front of the brightening glare, when she saw the granite eyes of the woman figure close its lids slowly and the remaining emerald light filter down to the base of the fossilized trunk, darkening the recesses of the room.

In a single moment, the man's eyes grew hot white, and a fraction before a heavy shift below them, the stare burst into solid streams of white condensed as solid as any laser. The stiff streams of shimmering pale energy connected with Jesse's gaze, sending a convulsing shock through his body, flooding his mind with information, and then throwing him back across the chamber in the darkness. Evelyn inhaled sharply with fear and instinctively sprung out from the illuminated holy ray from the heavens which bathed her. Her instincts drove her protectively to her love, and the eyes of the now-frozen standing stone fell dark and heavy.

XXIX

The Rising

Huge mountains of water rose along the eastern skyline of Peru as the continent shifted with an unknown force.

All across the world, seaside cities were experiencing devastating flooding and massive earthquakes. Central America was wrought with panic as residents of Costa Rica and El Salvador fled from the separating land bridge between the Americas. Buildings crumbled into the sea where continents tore themselves from their neighboring lands. The Earth had come alive again, and glaciers broke away from the poles as Antarctica moved toward its ancient companion, Australia.

The Great Pyramid that had once stood powerfully on the single landmass of God's creation was rising again. The capstones slid back as the massive structure moved from deep within the confines of the Earth, where God had imprisoned it millions of years ago. Twisting within the deep core of the Earth Mother, where the Tower connected with the centermost point of all of the land, each singular mass that had been pressed apart now drifted heavily back in on itself.

Power stations and military installations exploded, and planes fell from the sky as the electromagnetic pulse of the great shifting poles cut power across the globe. Species of every animal stampeded inward away from the windy shoals from the coming currents that would inevitably devastate the outermost reaches of the final vast island. The tsunamis generated from the rapid movement of the continents all advanced quickly toward the shores of Africa where the lands would eventually meet one another and force the torrents upward in a massive pinch.

The lands of Egypt, Sudan, Libya, Saudi Arabia, and surrounding countries were swallowed up in moments as the great Tower of Babel twisted its way toward the heavens.

From space, it was as if a massive upside-down cyclone had sucked the Great Pyramid out of the ground, and the continents of the Earth had been drawn into its rotating vortex. Crushing the innermost landmasses up above the churning seas' reach, the seams of the meeting continents exploded up with torrential amounts of water, so massive that no living thing would possibly survive its crushing weight as it returned to the Earth.

Movement settled as the peak of the rising tower touched the sky and drenches of settling water, larger than any country, flowed down the sloping sides of the Super Continent and back into the surrounding ocean, which had now been gathered together in one place.

A constant mist was hovering over the united globe as a fog does after a storm.

The sun had breached the horizon and the tiny drops of moisture caught and refracted the rays, sharing them with one another, and angling the light in a perfect rainbow of a size never beheld before.

On the eastern-most side, waves still broke heavily against the cliffs of Eurasia.

In the west, water lapped constantly upon the sandy shores of Pangea.

XXX
The Garden

Evelyn had gathered Jesse in her arms as the chamber shifted all around them. From above, the light had become a blaze of blinding white. Slowly adjusting the contrast in her eyes, she could see the blue of the sky an unspeakable distance above, like a tiny open eye on the heavens. At one point, she feared the interior walls of the room might collapse in on them as the sound of rock rubbed loudly while the whole monolith turned in its hugeness.

Even from this deep recess she could sense the changing Earth, and could hear the rush of sand and stone through the miles of thick wall between them and the surface. Evelyn pulled Jesse away from the wall of the chamber when she heard the stone upon sand get threateningly loud below them.

They sat inside the bounds of the flooded light from above as the floor opened up revealing a ten-foot-wide corridor of basalt steps leading downward. The steps had been there all along, yet the floor had rotated away to reveal them, and beyond was a distant light entering the depths of the steamy entrance.

Evelyn tried to rouse Jesse with all her might, but she only received a light plea to let him sleep. She tugged him up by the pullover sweat top, which tore under the strain. Stripping him of it, she tossed his arm over her shoulder and wrenched him to his feet. Half-dragging him, she made her way down the steps of the basalt case to the sunny open portal of the outside.

Taking the landing of the steps offered the warm rays of sunlight through a light haze of misty dew, which danced with colorful refraction all around them. A toucan cawed as its mate lit upon the branch of the giant Guava tree, burying its head in the cusp of the other's wing and preening. Beyond the landing of the stairs, yellowed stone turned to cleanly sifted soil trailing out into a vividly green carpet of ankle-high grasses. Drops of morning dew shimmered as they ran down the banana-leaved trees, whose trunks stood abundant with green and yellowed fruit, ripe for the picking.

Evelyn set Jesse down at the outermost reaches of the steps' flight, right on the edge of the terrace where he could rest, and she ventured quietly out onto the damp meadow, surveying from whence they had come.

The pyramid now stood as the most prominent and holy thing she had ever witnessed, its height unseen to the naked eye as it reached up in to the heavens beyond white wisps of cloud. Beyond it, past the lush, sparse foliage of this perfect scene of serenity, she saw a thing which brought her back to her senses, and released her from a bound mind. The snow-peaked cap of a distant volcano stood, steam still billowing from its chimney up into the stratus of the clouds above.

Evelyn thought of the flight with her mother, hand-in-hand around the massive smoldering volcano only nights before, but that had only been a dream, this was just as real as she now stood among the wet blades of moist saw-grass within this glade of perfect pleasure. She witnessed massive amounts of birds circling on the updrafts rounding that great peak, and also overhead of where she stood.

Yet more flocks of brilliant color were finding their ways to the remaining dry land of the world, seeking refuge in their huge formations among the glades.

A white, spotted fawn ate from the huckleberry growing at the edge of the meadow, beneath the shade of a Banyan tree, oblivious to (or unconcerned with) her presence.

Inside the chamber, the stone statues of immortal lovers still stood silently, wrapped in each other's arms before the great tree which now glistened naturally with the light from above. Despite the cloud cover, the golden rays still met their destination within, for the very peak of this astonishing tower pierced the highest clouds and drew in constant energy from the day. Yet outside, the wispy white of the sky still allowed no light to penetrate purely upon the great continent, since the miraculous raising of Babel.

It was only when Evelyn spied the mammoth stone of granite, bearing a giant graven symbol on its surface, that she thought of Adam. She momentarily reminisced into his faith, and nearly became overwhelmed with the story of the tree of good and evil.

It had been the time that the woman had partaken of the fruit of knowledge that paradise had been taken from them. In some way, she teared up within, thinking also of the consequence when man built the great tower to heaven, seeking more knowledge. She could see within her own soul now, beyond any doubt, that the true test of knowledge was not what we know how to do, but how we act when we do not know *what* to do.

On the surface of the great stone was the Holy Cross and from it a ray of gold was etched from its intersection reaching down to the left, and on the right was a mirror image, but of silver. A perfect circle rounded from the top of the apex of the three rays and completed the symbolic sign of union. Beneath the symbol, a simple axiom was engraved into the granite.

'What is bred in the bone, will come out in the flesh.'

And growing from the basalt itself that surrounded the depiction of the sign of unity, were budding sprouts of *her* very own tree of knowledge, the Oxychana plant.

Fruits of every variety riddled the impossibly beautiful grove: apples of red and gold, sweet and furry kiwi, grapefruit, cherry trees, even vines of cantaloupe twisted in the emerald sparkling grass. Never had Evelyn witnessed such a magnificent sight, and never had she felt as if she was being taken care of like she did now.

A strange calm came over her as she glanced back at where her Love lay, dozing lightly. She saw him, in all his glory, just as if they sat back in the hotel in London, and she thought of what he said that third night. She pondered the Oxychana that grew here, and the knowledge that may or may not lie within it for her, but she would never need it. Experience had given her knowledge enough, just as Jesse had said.

"Experience is not what happens to a man. It is what a man does with what happens to him."

What had happened here was no less than a miracle. She cried softly, watching as the stunning wildlife stirred amid the distant trees in harmony with one another. She had secretly prayed for this, in the Christian fashion, which was so unlike her.

Here she was on the brink of living the beautiful fantasy which had been laid out by her Adam so many years ago, as he explained his concept of creation. How she had longed, as deeply as in any child's imagination, to share that perfect garden called Eden with the one she loved for an eternity. Now, here she stood, and looking down at the convex line of her abdomen, she wept in praise.

The man on the basalt steps stirred, first very subtly and then, opening his eyes on the shimmering colors of the misty glade, was sure he was seeing Heaven. He wore a pair of earth-stained sweats and sandals, and his chest was bare in the warmth of the air.

He stood to his feet, now hungry for what looked to be some of the freshest fruits hanging from trees beneath the colored wings of preening birds. There was no anxiety in his movements, no haste in any step or action that he took. He felt at peace, as if he had awakened from a dream into another dream and knew that he was safe from harm.

'The lushness of this place is beyond measure,' he thought to himself, his feet groping at the damp grassy floor of the grove while he crossed.

A yellow jaguar scaled the crooked branches of an oak, and a peacock chortled from behind a thickly woven fern, only the eyes of its feathers peeking from behind the foliage. A slowly lumbering sloth peered out with hazel eyes from among the leaves of a mountain Soursop, pinched in its mouth a sprig of fresh green branch of fig.

Reaching up, Jesse took a single guava from a branch, and the resplendent birds perched there ignored him in his innocence, as he sank his teeth into its juicy, tender flesh. Pink juice rolled from the corner of his mouth, and he praised the Earth for her abundant pleasures.

'The beauty of this place could not be surpassed in many lifetimes, may I never awaken from this dream,' he told himself as he began to indulge in the flesh of the sweet fruit, once again.

But he was wrong, for he now spied *her*, a creature of even further indescribable beauty, clad in leather-beaded skins, covering only the most particular parts of her grandeur.

The guava fell from his limp hand, landing on the velveteen carpet of grass, as she approached him.

The cloudy rooftop of the world finally opened up its heart upon the land and a ray of spiritual golden light broke through the first porthole of the ceiling. The beam cast down beside the couple as Evelyn's hands glided softly up the smooth creamy contour of the man's chest, who she had only known as Jesse. His eyes verified her momentary fear, but her mind again heard the echoing word of his within.

'Experience is not what happens to a man. It is what a man does with what happens to him.'

The man's eyes were a mesmerizing blue, full of mischief and grandeur. She stared, for a moment and then, as if taking command of an unmanned vessel, she spoke to him.

"Welcome to our Eden, my love."

The man didn't ask the questions which were pressing at him gently in this moment, but instead watched her lips as they came to his in gentle love, her hand clasping his to her chest. This place, this feeling, this beauty causing emotional blindness, which clouded his every thought, was all he needed. But there was one question he knew he *must* ask. He must know her name. What should he call this lovely thing into which he had already become so immersed?

The skies opened as Evelyn turned beside him, laying her head upon his shoulder and gazing out toward the majestic line of treetops, which cradled the looming volcano above. Glancing up at him, she saw his lips come to life with speech.

"You say this place is Eden. It is a garden ... beauty like I have never seen. But I must know what name has the Creator given the most beautiful lady who dominates this glade?" His eyes went shallow in thought for a moment before he asked, with a bit more touch of concern, "And oddly, I must know, who I am to be in such a place as this? Do I have a name?"

She poised herself, for the moment, burning it deep into her memory, as Jesse once did, and then answered.

"You are *my* Adam," she said, smiling at that small thought and word.

"And I ..." Her breath escaped her lips with all intentions of offering her full name to him, but her tongue stopped short as the Light of Heaven broadened over the Holy Couple and out into the reaches of the land beyond.

"Eve."

As a gift from the Father, Jesse's memories came flooding back ...

"And the trees awoke and knew them,
and the wild things gathered to them,
as they kissed amongst the wooded glen,
love growing manifold."

Epilogue:
Mother Earth Speaks

It was over the surface of the deep that my curiosity began. From my own Waters did I create the Fire, which would drive the engine of creation and allow myself to experience my own magnificence. But, in my vanity, there was a flaw. Because every single piece of life that was myself had formed on the same principles, each piece would, in turn, possess the same curiosity of their origin that drove me within to seek it, and this I could not have known.

It was the first bite of the forbidden fruit that threw the peace into turmoil. I should have seen the flaw, but I did not. On and on my people pressed and grew in worship, grasping at any belief or deity in hopes of finding natural balance once again. But even when every man came together with a single purpose and voice, it was not to enjoy more fully the unlimited life and knowledge they possessed, but rather to acquire more knowledge, and none existed.

A million years they built, with the unlimited power granted them by an unimaginably unlimited God. The very stones, which were bones of the earth, and soil my flesh, could be moved with the slightest effort. For faith was not lacking in the New World. Mountains were hewn and unhewn with nothing more than prayer. But even this boundless freedom they possessed couldn't push the single splinter from their minds as a people. The need for more, was a thing I had birthed deep within each of my children, and was something I could not easily temper and extract from them.

It was not until the tower was completed from my own flesh and bone, created to soak up the power of my depths, draw down the light of the Creator and imbue a watcher with its ultimate knowledge, that I beg the Father act. This single act of devastation to our own bodies of creation was a necessary experience to the growth process. Giving man in all of his glory, the full understanding of his power was far too dangerous to do in a single instant. Becoming aware is a thing that takes millennia to achieve. The Father and I have patiently waited through the enduring processes time and time again, but this we did on our own.

Man was different, for he came forth in abundance, and the brilliant minds of spiritual children were blind to the miracle of what they had already come to achieve with but minimum effort on their own part. Because the child feels as if they played no role in their own amazing creation, they will seek to *do* and to *know* more, unconscious of the fact that they have already helped make miracles. It was only through time that we could allow our offspring the ultimate realization that creation is a triune process. As the three rays shine from the sun, so do the three elements imbue one another with the gift of life.

The Father's Love, the Mother's Body, and the Child's Will. Just as moon reflects the sun upon the earth, this triune is also apparent in the seasons of birth, life, and death. One grants power to another, it is a cycle, and an upward climb, which we have been hiking in an eternal journey for the plateau atop which beckons us.

In his own ignorance did early man seek out the thing he already owned and most coveted ... yet he simply did not take responsibility for its possession. And so, in a grand effort, the Father cast the heavenly temple down into the center of the once unified land of man, segregating the continents and the languages, abashing man's wasted efforts to gain knowledge of the unknown. True knowledge comes from within, and to tap it, one need only know oneself. Complete universal knowledge, granted to a person from an outside source, would only cause total memory loss for they would expect every answer to exist beyond their eternal reach, and their life would become a constant question.

As the Earth Mother, I am with my children along every step of the way and experience fully the emotion and growth of the people. But the Heavenly Father reminds us in our actions, on a daily basis, that the miracle of life on which we have worked countless eons to create has not come about to ask the question:

"How did *I* come to be?"

But rather to question in the spirit and amazement of an innocent child:

"Now that we have achieved this amazing miracle, what together, shall we do next?!"

The Father Speaks

It is the general way of things, ebb and flow. In and out, up and down, back and forth, right to left, black and white, good and bad, and on and on—these are the opposites. Too many times have I looked upon my reflection as I hovered over the surface of the deep, and expected that image to make me change. Millennia passed before it would ever slightly move my hand, and this was only after I had let the image looking back at me grow old and tired. Was youth my motivation to go within and seek more for myself?

Perhaps.

But in the end, it was I who called upon the beginning by reflecting on what I had experienced. It was I who questioned my past memories. It was I who faltered, and it was I who rose again. It was I who was fluent before being gifted with speech. It was I who was a drop in the air. It was I who was set adrift on a boundless sea, and it was I that grew for nine months in the womb.

It was I that kindled fire in the head. It was I that singly built the Tower of Babel. It was I that doubted, and had forgotten, calling myself in the darkness.

Yes, and it was I who saw myself from the reflection of the mirror and only vaguely found the image familiar. And it was I who lived to experience every corner of emotion, from happiness to greed and back, to loss and regret.

It was I who questioned them. It was I who sought an answer to why it was that they'd forsaken me. And it was I who'd forgotten the face of my father.

But in the end, when the brooding darkness enveloped me, I would again see his face, which was my own. For the one thing I had left to gain, was the one thing that had made the journey possible. I had made … Forgetting—and *by* forgetting it—experienced the remembrance of myself through you … and in turn, my own magnificence.

And it was in this hour that the Father cried out from within.

"It is you!"

And finally it was I who dared to hear, and realize, that it was always me. And it was I who found myself asking myself back again:

"Who but I can let known the secrets of the unhewn dolmen?"
"Who but I can know the mystery of the moon?"
"Who but I can find the secret resting place of the sun?"
And finally,
"Who but I can now decide where this life will take me?"

Who but I?
Who but you?

The End

Thank You for Enjoying Eve, the second book in the Pangea Chronicles, by Jay M. Horne.
Find other great titles and updated news about the prequel and sequel at the publisher's website.

www.bookflurry.com

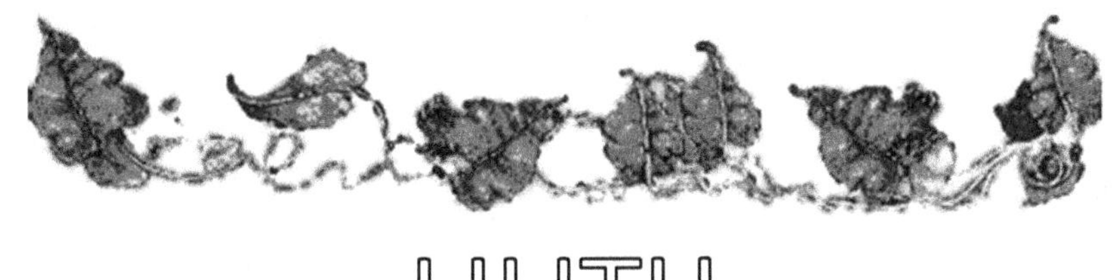

LILITH

The First Book in the Pangea Chronicles

CHAPTER ONE

Stardust

The speed of light could only be defined by the particles that itself was yet to reveal. In the instant after the big bang, light had not had time to shine upon any particles. 'Twas only stardust that spewed forth from the singularity. Thus, no definition bound those particles to neither scrutiny of law nor judgement. In the expanding and drifting aftermath of the molten explosion, no terms could shed light upon the world that would be known as 'The World of Form'.

Only 'The World of Force' existed in the very first moments—a dark, lonely void—that fought to catch up with the horizon of light that raced into the beyond.

To those who dwelt in that void, it was they who cast the first stone of creation into the murky depths of the sea of potential; the ripples of that stone manifesting the reality of the world that would come as the light dawned on the world of the living.

The Mother Speaks

"Everything is opposite in the spirit world. Duality is considered only a means to define forces at work in the shifting ether of the formless world of ideas and dreams. Much as the seed bears the weight of the entire make-up of the mighty oak at its center—so does the simple singularity bear the weight of the world—sprouting forth, only after being plunged into utter darkness.

"Like attracts like in this world of pure force. Electrons seek electrons on the outskirts of the primordial soup, and protons whir in the first music of the electromagnetic spectrum as they daringly dance with neutrons in these first moments of our existence. Feminine energies have bonded with feminine energies and male's with male's, both oblivious—until now—of one another."

There was no connection to be *known* to one another in the world of potential, it could only be *felt*; the feeling only fleeting as potential ideas and dreams collided in the ultimate sea of the deep. Each piece of fluxing energy was a radiant orb of potential much like a stone poised atop a hill, waiting for a gentle breeze to set it into motion—an orgasm at its apex but never released.

The Maiden Speaks

"Oh, Mother ... the exquisite yet divine torture of this feeling of growth and consciousness. It is unbearable among this dancing miasma of imagination. I know our beauty, I LOVE our beauty. I sense the coalition of the waters that are us, drawing together in one place and the fires of a divine one's will drawing together in another place. How I long to drink of those waters, to take them into me. To know what it FEELS like to be my own magnificence."

But, this she could not do. The act of 'feeling' was in the masculine, yet the masculine had no art of 'the imagination' and it was in that gift alone that the masculine endured the inferno that was the coalescing of fire, opposite the feminine world of force. Had they the ability to imagine the destructive potential which their fires held, the masculine would surely have snuffed itself out among the pain.

It was in the moment of the Mother's realization of these opposing forces that the Maiden asked the simple question that would change their worlds forever; a question which could only be answered by the Crone who dwelt in the beyond.

"How did we become so separated from the masculine?"

The Crone Speaks

"Ah, the origins of duality is a definition that is not easily understood. For in the world that is, nothing can be undone. All that is, is all there ever was, and there is nothing else. We are that we are. There is no way to undo the pure knowingness of our existence, which we experience as ultimate pleasurable imagination. Time is a thing that beckons even the world of the Fae, yet its ability to change us is lessened. This is why in our imagination lies our despair. For even as we marvel at our own potential beauty, we weep with want for the ability to FEEL it, and this we cannot do without first experiencing our opposite, which is dark and *painful*."

The last word was amiss of meaning to the Mother and Maiden, though it stirred curiosity.

"The experience and thus the knowingness of this darkness is essential to Feeling. How can you weigh your pleasure if you know not *pain*?"

Again, the word was amiss to the Divine Beings who dwelt in the Void of Force.

Yet again, it was the Maiden who questioned, "How then do I experience this pain? When there is not but what is already here, and there will be nothing else, how then do I ever experience the Feeling of our magnificence?"

At this, a dry cackle permeated the world of the Fae.

"Therein lies the conundrum. The experience of yourself, you have already had. It lies within. All possibility has been done. The illusion is that you have not yet journeyed into the flesh, yet how then does your imagination writhe with exquisite experiences, which tease you into near ecstasy? I say, *you have lived them*. You are that you are and there is no way to be other than *that*. Though, you *have* left yourself a gift, which only *I* can bestow to you. You have only to but ask."

With this the Mother's voice rises above the other aspects of the Triune Self and pleads to the Maiden's lustfulness, "I caution you to be happy with what is. What gain is there in wanting, child? The very act itself is an expression of lack."

The Mother cannot harken to the Maiden for the Mother is peace in itself; in her purest form—*that* is what she is—Peace. She knows she cannot sway the Maiden—and the Maiden's strongest attribute is her allure—so it would be futile and unnecessary.

"The mother will always be here for you. In your darkest time, call out, and I will lift you up to my divine light once more."

It was in this time—a time after all time—that the Crone bestowed upon the Maiden the gift of *forgetting* ... the only thing that would shatter the infinite knowledge of existence into a mighty array of pieces, which would take lifetimes to put together and RE-MEMBER.

And as does a seed, she called upon herself the darkness and went within ... her first memory—Water.

Keep a look-out for the Prequel to 'EVE'. 'LILITH'—due for publication by 2020 and the sequel 'ADAM'—due for publication by 2023.

The Pangea Chronicles came to life in Book Two, EVE, with Jesse and Evelyn finding their way to one another with the help of the Fae and the Djinn. The Tower has been resurrected and Adam, the child of the divine couple, grows within Eve's womb.

Read 'Lilith' and journey back to the beginning, when the Fae world took its first breath just after the initial blast that created the universe. Meet the beings of the world before life, before substance, whose thoughts mold the reality of what is to come in the world of form. See what mistakes the Creators may have made had they ever had the ability to form a wrong thought.

In the sequel 'ADAM', delve into the mind of the creator come to Earth, caught between destiny and reality. Can he make a wrong choice? Does anyone ever have a choice at all in the world of the living? Does the choices he's made in the world of the Time make him who he is to become, or do the choices he makes as a human change the destiny he has already written himself?

Read more 'Chronicles of Pangea' philosophy, editor's cuts, and exclusive interviews, and get book related merchandise at the Chronicle's of Pangea Facebook Fan page.

https://www.facebook.com/ChroniclesofPangea

www.ingramcontent.com/pod-product-compliance
Lightning Source LLC
Chambersburg PA
CBHW060603310726
48982CB00008B/1222/J